FOR THOSE ABOUT TO READ, WE SALUTE YOU!

ABOUT THE SPARTAPUSS SERIES...

"Cattastic" – LONDON EVENING STANDARD

"Non-stop adventure... Spartapuss serves notice that cattitude rules!" – I LOVE CATS (USA)

"It's Rome AD36 and the mighty Feline Empire rules the world. This is the diary of slave cat Spartapuss, who finds himself imprisoned and sent off to gladiator school to learn how to fight, for fight he must if he wants to win his freedom. Packed with more catty puns than you ever thought pawsible, this witty Roman romp is history with cattitude." – SCHOLASTIC JUNIOR MAGAZINE

"Spartapuss makes history fun instead of dull...For people who don't like history (like me), this book might change their minds." – SHRUTI PATEL, AGED 10

"I really enjoyed this book and I liked the fact that it was written as if it was Spartapuss's diary. My favourite character was Russell (a crow!!!) Spartapuss's friend. I would recommend this book for ages 10+ especially if you enjoy books with a twist and a sense of humour."
– SAM (11-YEAR-OLD YOUNG ARCHAEOLOGIST MEMBER FROM YORK)

"Catligula's reign, a time when cats ruled Rome, was short if bloody, a story told by freedcat Spartapuss, employed as a scribe by Catligula, whose life was saved by Spartapuss.
The Emperor is mad, poisoning those he believes to be his enemies and making his pet, Rattus Rattus, a member of the Senate. The Spraetorian Guard are determined to end his reign before Catligula ruins the empire.

Based loosely upon the writings of classical historians, Catligula is the second in a series that re-tells the scandals of the early Caesars in an accessible form, inevitably reminiscent of Robert Graves' *I, Claudius*. The jokes lie mainly in the names – the Greeks become Squeaks – but the descriptions of life in classical Rome are good, particularly the set piece in the Arena, when Catligula plays himself in what must have been an embarrassing display to even his sycophantic feline audience.

Readers who know the original stories will enjoy the fun, and those who don't know the history may be enticed to look more closely at the Roman stories."
– THE SCHOOL LIBRARIAN, VOL 53 NO 4, 2005

"This is too good to be left just as a children's book! Extremely funny and brilliantly written. Robin Price has taken the events of Roman history focusing around the time of Emperors Tiberious, Caligula and Claudius and turned it into something fascinating."
– MONSTERS AND CRITICS.COM

"I would recommend them... Thrillers that you can't put down 'til you've read the whole thing."
– FIONA MURRAY THE JOURNAL OF CLASSICS TEACHING

To Jonathan

CLEOCATRA'S KUSHION

ROBIN PRICE

MOGZILLA

CLEOCATRA'S KUSHION

First published by Mogzilla in 2010

Paperback edition:
ISBN: 978-1-906132-06-4

Hardback edition:
ISBN: 978-1-906132-07-1

www.mogzilla.co.uk

Printed and bound in the UK by CPI Mackays, Chatham ME5 8TD

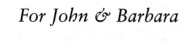

For John & Barbara

THE TALE SO FAR...

CLEOCATRA'S CUSHION is the fifth book in the SPARTAPUSS series. It's set in an ancient Roman world ruled by cats, where humans have never existed.

In I AM SPARTAPUSS, SPARTAPUSS is comfortable managing Rome's finest Bath and Spa. He is a loyal servant to his master CLAWDIUS – a cat of the Imperial Family. But Fortune has other plans for him. There is a nasty incident in the vomitorium. It causes offence to CATLIGULA the would-be heir to the cushioned throne. SPARTAPUSS is thrown into prison, only to be released into gladiator training school. At the end of his training, he is given a golden coin by his mentor TEFNUT. He fights at the Games and is freed by CATLIGULA. CLAWDIUS is angry because he has lost a valuable slave. Shortly afterwards, SPARTAPUSS rescues CATLIGULA from a chariot crash.

In the second book in the series, CATLIGULA becomes Emperor and his madness brings Rome to within a whisker of disaster. The SPRAETORIAN GUARD plot to get rid of him and need SPARTAPUSS to help. SPARTAPUSS agrees but at the last minute changes his mind and helps CATLIGULA to escape. He convinces the Emperor that he is needed to perform a play. During the show, the Arena is flooded in mysterious circumstances and CATLIGULA is lost. The Emperor's guards look for revenge for the death of their master. They find CLAWDIUS (CATLIGULA's uncle) hiding on a cupboard. On SPARTAPUSS'S suggestion, they announce that CLAWDIUS is the new Emperor of the Known World.

In DIE CLAWDIUS, the third book in the series, CLAWDIUS decides to invade SPARTAPUSS'S home land – The Land of the Kitons. SPARTAPUSS is forced to join the first ship of the invasion fleet. Shortly after landing, he is captured by a hostile tribe. He escapes into the woods where he meets FURG, a young Kiton studying to become a MEWID. Angry at the Roman invaders, FURG storms off to join the rebels. SPARTAPUSS decides to stay and look for her.

In BOUDICAT, the fourth book in the series, eighteen years have passed since the invasion. Spartapuss, like many other Roman settlers, has become rich. With his wife away in Rome, Spartapuss is asked to deliver a message to her aunt, QUEEN BOUDICAT. When the warrior queen learns of the Emperor's plans to rob her of her kingdom, she goes on the war path. In the course of the rebellion, SPARTAPUSS loses everything but he is given QUEEN BOUDICAT'S priceless silver torc necklace as a gift. He sets sail for Rome to join his wife and son with a large bag of gold.

DRAMATIS PAWSONAE

Who's who

From the jungles of Catage to the forests of Purrmania, The Feline Empire rules the known world. Ships sail from the Roman port of Ostia to the Land of the Furraohs and up the river Nile to the Kingdom of the Kushionites.

The Romans:

Nero – Emperor of Rome.
Spitulus – 'The Educated Gladiator' now retired and working for Nero.
Purris – an actor and one time friend of the Emperor, now in prison.
Eddipuss – a unlicensed cart driver.

The Kitons:

Spartapuss (The Elder) – a ginger cat from the Land of the Kitons. Now married with a son.
Son of Spartapuss (S.O.S.) – a young Kiton, who has come to Rome for the first time.

The Kushionites and Others:

Haireena – the daughter of a fish seller.
Misis – the daughter of a cook from the Land of Misr (called 'Fleagypt' by the Romans).
Queen Kandmeet – the ruler of the Kushionites.
Jebel – a frog.

Dear FATHER,

Hail from the capital of the mighty Feline
Empire.

Rome is big but it's not anything like
you said. Your favourite temples are looking all tatty. The Romans aren't much
good at stone carving either. The head of
Hercatlules, the God of the Gladiators, is
far too big for his body. He looks like he's
carrying a shopping bag, not a lion skin.

Yours,

S.O.S.

P.S. Please send more gold because I'm
running out. I need to buy that present for
mother and get tickets for the Emperor's
festival.

CATILIS XXVII
July 27th

I write from my cabin as we approach the port of Ostia. It is a joy to be travelling in comfort for a change. I say 'comfort' although my back paws are giving me the usual trouble. I must go to the healer and get something for them.

The fish on board is of the best quality. Except the mackerel – which is an nasty bony fish, however fine the sauce.

Who'd ever think that I would be returning to Rome as a freedcat? And as a cat of considerable riches! Queen Boudicat's torc collar turned out to be made of highest grade silver. It started a bidding war between two traders from Maul. This ended in hisses but thankfully did not come to claws. Must go now as I need to unpack and count my money.

CATILIS XXVIII
July 28th

News of terrible woe! On unpacking my luggage, I noticed that there is a hole in one of my money bags. Luckily, it is a small hole and my gold coins are very large – so none of them have fallen out. Thank Peus that I have luck of the rich – for smaller coins would have dropped straight through the hole.

My fellow travellers are all tourists and talk of little except shopping. The port of Ostia is but a flea's jump from Rome and it is a gathering point for all the traders of the Empire. You can buy: 'fine pottery from Maul'; (cracked) 'wild beasts from Catage' (tame or sick) and 'treasures from Fleagypt' (cursed by the Furroahs, most likely).

They are also selling 'silver from the master smiths of the Land of the Kitons'. I've warned the tourists not to believe this. Back at home they give the title of 'master smith' to any cat who turns up to work by noon and can hold a hammer the right way round.

I got another letter from my son today:

Dear Father,

Hail and all of that. Thanks for the money you sent. I didn't get mother a golden bowl like you said, because my lyre needed new strings. They must have got wet on the ship. Rusty strings are no good for my image as The Lord of the Lyre from Land of Kitons. You'll find a present for mother in Ostia. It is said that they've got a market there. It's the biggest in the Feline Empire, so even you should be able to find her something.
Yours,

S.O.S.

CATILIS XXIX

July 29th

News of considerable annoyance! Another third letter has just arrived:

Dear Father,

> *Tragic news! The tickets for the Emperor's festival have all sold out. Send a faster crow next time. And sacrifice something to Fortuna or one of the other gods. I am off to write a sad song about it now.*
> *Yours in sadness,*
> *S.O.S.*

P.S.
> *Snapped new strings. Please send more gold.*

I fear I must join the tourists on a shopping trip to the market. My son has failed to find a present for his mother, even though the task involved spending my money. I have hired a crow to send word that I have arrived. I've sent more gold too, as he asked. But this is the very last time. He'll need more than new strings for that cursed lyre of his, if he is going to win a singing contest. Poor S.O.S. could not carry a tune in a bucket. Not even a golden one!

AUGUSTPUSS II

August 2nd

Ruined

Iam ruined. Oh Caturn, Lord of Time – with your sickle dangling from your back! If only you could make the water run back up the waterclock. Or chase the shadow backwards round the sundial's face. You do not have to give me back my gold, so cruelly tricked from my paws. But I beg you to send back my foolish son, who has been taken away from me.

The tale begins in the Ostia's market – a meeting place for traders from all corners of the Feline empire, and half the tourists too by the smell of it. In the hot crush, they fought over the souvenirs. I scoured this battlefield with weary pads in search of new bags for my money and a present for my wife.

I was making my way towards a trader selling animal skins from Catage, when some unusual vases caught my eye, as did the seller. Her coat was dark and thick and she had honey-coloured eyes that would have held me like a goat on a lead. I admired her impressive pots for a while before she called me over, holding up a black jar with holes around the rim.

"This one is for you sir. It's very fine. See how it catches the light."

Saying this, she flicked it gently with a delicate paw and set it spinning. As it began to turn, the flame of her lamp shone through holes around the rim.

"This one is very lucky. It is said a pot from the land of the Kushionites will always lead you to good fortune."

"I very much doubt that!" I replied.

"By Queen Kandmeet, I swear it's true. Because if you buy this one today, I'll give you a second one for free."

I mewed in horror – not at her sales talk but because I could feel something wet and slimy on my tail. I leapt back and began to search frantically for a stick to prod the horrid creature with. But the seller begged me to stop.

"Don't mind little Jebel," she said. "You've got to keep a frog with you if you want good luck."

Disgusted, I padded away from the stall. For a frog is not the sort of creature that a Roman would call a pet. Not even the worst barbarian from Maul would keep one, except as an ingredient for one of his sauces.

"Come back!" called the seller. I shook my head and padded off with a swish of the tail. But to my surprise, she leapt right over her counter and started to follow me through the market.

"Need any help?" asked a voice at my side.

"Not today thank you!" I said, not liking the look of him. "Or tomorrow either," I added.

He was a wire-haired creature who looked as if someone had given him the Lean and Hungry

Cookbook for his birthday.

Taking me aside, the fellow said in a loud voice that on no account should a noble Roman like me let these foreign demons get the better of him. This whole market was a den of thieves, full of suspicious types from Fleagypt and places even worse than that. It was a nest of vipers.

I pointed out that vipers do not live in nests. He ignored this, begging that if I would only allow him to speak on my behalf, I would get a better bargain. For he was not only a cart driver, but also a driver of bargains. I was about to tell him exactly where he could park his cart when a voice called:

"Wait! It is a pot of the highest quality!"

It was the vase seller, who'd caught up with me.

"Silence female. A Roman needs silence when he's making his noble mind up," hissed the fellow, in rather a rude manner.

"RICHES! It will bring you GREAT RICHES," cried the seller, ignoring him.

"For Peus sake, will you BOTH be quiet?" I begged. "I already have great riches. Actually, I was going to use your pot to put my great riches in. There is a hole in one of my money bags. Is it impossible to find a simple bag anywhere in this market?"

This got the driver excited, for he sprang up onto the board of an empty stall and made a speech.

"SILENCE all of you. Be quiet and listen to the Romans. This fellow here, a citizen no doubt, has a great deal of money – and needs to buy some big bags to keep it in! If there is a bag seller amongst you please come forward now! The rest of you Fleagyptians, just go about your businesses and keep your noses out."

I felt the eyes of the whole crowd upon me and heard the pot seller gasp.

"By Amun's Fleece! Do you want to start a riot? You cannot let your driver insult them like that!" she cried.

"That fellow is not my driver," I protested.

"He should not have called them Fleagyptians. That was very dangerous and I fear they may fall upon him like a pack of wolves on a lone sheep."

And as she was speaking, a crowd of traders with sandy coloured coats sprang forth and squared up to Eddipuss (for that was troublesome driver's name).

"I don't think he meant to insult them," I began. "Are they not from the Land of Fleagypt?"

"SHUSH!" commanded the seller. "Do not say that word in here if you value your ginger hide."

As she spoke, I had a horrible vision of my fur being taken and used as the fringing on a cushion! Looking around me I saw plenty of stalls selling that kind of thing.

By now a war was breaking out between three attackers. Eddipuss knocked the first two down with a caldron – but as he was warning the third, I felt a claw dig into my own chest.

"You owe us Roman," cried a voice. "Look at the

damage your driver has caused!" Then he let out a hiss like a basket of snakes. At least I thought it was him hissing – but I turned out to be standing next to a snake seller's stall.

"He owes you nothing, you son of a sheep!" cried Eddipuss. "Be gone or I will unleash the Furries themselves upon you!"

The snake seller leapt to the attack and a furious battle began. Unable to leave for fear of a bite – I decided to have a few friendly words with the pot seller.

"Many apologies if I have offended you. How should I call those from Fle… I mean from the Land of the mighty river Nile and Queen Cleocatra?"

The pottery seller smiled.

"You have not offended me. The name of that land is 'Misr'. But half the traders in this market are not from Misr – they are Kushionites, like me."

The crowd were enjoying the battle between Eddipuss and the snake seller. In fact, Eddipuss was getting a lot of support.

"Most Kushionites have little love for the Fleagyptians," she purred. "You should hear what some of them call us."

"Kushionites eh? What brings you to Ostia?"

"We come to trade. Cushions from Kush are famous all throughout the Empire. I'll show you."

She disappeared for a short time before returning with a beautiful purple cushion. It was the softest thing that I have ever felt.

"I'll take it," I said. "I need a gift for my wife. And give me those pots while you are at it!"

As she got the coins in her paw, Eddipuss appeared with the furious snake seller on his tail. He leapt onto the stall opposite and began to throw caldrons, bronze mirrors and other gifts at his opponent.

The wizened caldron seller leapt at Eddipuss and joined forces with the snake-seller. The crowd began to cheer as the old one raked at Eddipuss with his sharpened claws.

Poor Eddipuss was cornered, but he refused to be beaten. In a rage, he snatched up a large leather bag and began to empty it into the crowd.

There came a dreadful gasp. A writhing knot of angry snakes fell from the bag and began to slither in all directions. It started a general panic.

I have a horror of snakes. I lay still as Mewpiter's statue as the terrible things came towards me. Eddipuss ignored the hisses and stuffed the bag over the snake seller's head, tying it with a snake-buckle belt.

"Come on!" he cried, grabbing the pots and the cushion from my shaking paws. "To your cart! And let us be quick about it."

"But I don't have a cart," I protested.

"Don't worry," said Eddipuss. "You can hire mine."

THE SECRET DIARY OF S.O.S.

Day I

She's so beautiful. When I saw her on the Senate steps, I took her for the daughter of a senator. It turns out that her father is a fish seller. At least, I think that's what he is – he was carrying a big bucket of crabs when he came to pick her up. I'm trying to write a song about her, but my paws shake when I touch the frets. I don't know her name, so I'm calling her 'Cleocatra'.

> Cleocatra – *with your long dark coat,*
> Cleocatra – *come and give me a stroke,*
> Cleocatra – *what a perfect dish,*
> *twice as sweet as your father's fish.*

I practiced the last verse for three hours last night but had to give up when the shouting from the street grew too loud. Some cats in this city have no taste in music.

Day II

Well diary – I've done it. Today I spoke to her! I was going to sing my new song but my paws were shaking so much, I couldn't get the case of my lyre undone. I tried to tell her about my love. But the words didn't come out right.

"Fair one! Wait!" I called. "If I was a sailor, I'd sail a thousand miles for you. If I was a doctor, I'd make you better. If I made jewellery, I'd make you a collar. But I'm not any of those things…"

"You're not much use then," she laughed. "It's a good job that I'm not sick. Luckily I don't need any new jewellery either."

My heart nearly cracked. Was that it? Were we going to pass like rats in the night?

"Going to Paws field to watch the Emperor pass by tomorrow?" I asked casually, knowing that all the females love a good military parade.

"Perhaps," she replied.

"Great. See you on the steps tomorrow at noon," I called. "Wait – I don't know your name!"

But she was already gone. I begged a nearby fish seller to tell me all he knew of her, and he agreed – at a price. The old crook made me buy a fish for each piece of information.

"That one? With the dark fur?" he asked.

"That's her," I replied.

"That'll be half a degnawrius," he said, dumping a haddock at my feet.

"Paw's jaws! That's not fair! You haven't told me anything yet. What's her name? Where's she from?"

"She's a Kushionite," he replied.

"Watch what you say," I bristled, "Speak ill of her, and I swear it will go very badly for you."

"She's a Kushionite," he laughed. "That means she's from the Land of Kush. Where in Paw's name did they drag you up?"

"In a village, in the Land of the Kitons," I answered.

"I thought so. A village full of idiots was it?" He laughed and threw a couple of crabs on the ground before me. Then he charged me another three degnawri.

"Her name's Haireena," he said, counting his money. "Isn't she a bit old to be your girlfriend?"

Now, I could have settled it with claws, but he might know her father. I'm already at an age where if I was a Roman, I would get to wear the collar of cathood. It's just a collar but it means you get to sit with the grown ups at restaurants. Father doesn't want me to wear one. He says that I'll only pay double for meals wearing that around my neck. He is always thinking of money, my father.

But where can I take her? It must be a date fit for the goddess Fleanus herself! I shall have a short nap and think about it. Meanwhile, I've worked all night on changing the words to her song. Not many words rhyme with Haireena.

Hair-reena – with your thick black ruff
Hair-reena – am I good enough?
Hair-reena – what a perfect dish
Hair-reena – sweet as your father's fish
Hair-reena – climbing up that tree
If I was a mouse, I'd let you play with me!

Day III

This morning I went back to the *Fatted Carp* cookshop. Now, you might wonder why I'd ignore my father and set paw in a place like that.

Ever since the day I arrived in Rome, I have heard nothing but tales about the Emperor Nero. It is said that his mules walk on silver shoes and he always goes fishing with a golden net. And he's building a Golden House that is a mile long with a fishing lake inside it!

So I started thinking – Haireena would love to visit it. They don't sell tickets for the Golden House. But one of the cats in the Fatted Carp is in charge of a gang who are blasting out the foundations. They call him 'the Capo'. I asked if he could get us in.

"That's impossible amici," said the Capo. "Nobody gets inside."

"Too bad, that's where I'm taking Haireena."

"Haireena eh?" he said.

"Yes – it's a beautiful name isn't it? It's probably foreign. It means something pretty, like 'flower'".

"It's an old Catin name," said the Capo. "It means 'sand'. And it'll be blood and sand for you two – if you go anywhere near Caesar's Golden Palace."

"There must be a way to get in," I pleaded.

"Forget it. Or it'll be this for you." He made the 'jugulare' – the claw across the throat gesture.

"Haireena," laughed a thin tabby. "I think I bought a haddock from her last week."

This got howls of laughter from the crowd.

Ignoring him, I reached into my bag and brought out one of the large gold coins that father had sent by crow.

"Would this change your mind Capo?" I asked. He cackled like a jackal.

"Golden love eh? Well, I'll need two of those to get you in – one for you and one for the fish-seller."

"Her name's Haireena,' I hissed. "And it's her father that sells fish, actually."

"What a waste of money," laughed an old tabby. "Why don't you take her down the fish market instead? She might get you a discount."

I was about to leap at the stranger's throat but the Capo held me back.

"Haireena is a princess, from the Land of Kush, actually. So I'm taking her on a date that's fit for a princess! We'll fall in love in the Golden House."

There was more laughter from the room.

"The Emperor might be there to see it," I boasted. "He might even give us his blessing."

"Have you got nothing at all but fur in that ginger head of yours? The Emperor hasn't moved in yet. It's death to look at him or speak unless you are spoken too," hissed the Capo.

"Any price is worth paying for Haireena."

"Well listen to me, my ginger cousin. You'd better follow my instructions, or your first date may be your last. Understand?"

AUGUSTPUSS X

August 10th

I was soon to learn that things have a habit of going wrong when you travel with Eddipuss.

He led me through streets so narrow that a rat could not run in them. On we went, until the pain from my pads became unbearable. We padded deep into the very worst part of town, passing cook shops serving rotten dormice, where even the mangy fear to tread. At last we came upon a wrecked cart.

A sign upon it read:

"Hire this vehicle and the driver.
Only VIII degnawri a day.
Plus food for the dog."

"This is a day, you'll thank almighty Peus for!" cried Eddipuss, loading the things upon the cart. "For it is the day when you met the best driver in Ostia. Where shall it be? To Rome? My dog looks old, but she has a lot of running in her. She's especially good at running away from me. I need a small advance for meat and biscuits."

"Where's my cushion?" I asked.

"Down there by your pots," he called, whistling through yellow teeth for his cart dog.

"That is not my cushion. Mine was a lovely purple

colour. That one is as brown as a bad supper and it stinks to the heavens. Peus knows what's been sitting on it!"

"Those Fleagyptian fools! They're a nation with sand in between their ears. They've mixed up your goods with someone else's. But perhaps Fortune has smiled on you Lord, for this cushion is far better than that purple one. Look! The stuffing is coming out. That is the mark of a true antique, is it not?"

It was pointless to argue.

I decided not to trust Eddipuss to drive me to Rome. I'd already made up my mind before I saw Caesar, his old bent-backed dog. It looked as if it couldn't pull the lid off a potted lobster. Then, a lucky spin by Fortune – we got stuck behind a lobster cart, which led us all the way back to the port.

It was with some relief when we drew up alongside my lodgings. I knew there would be an argument, so I pressed a golden coin into his paw (I had nothing smaller) and told him not wait for me. The sight of the gold shut him up, but his crooked dog would not stop howling as I went inside.

"I will settle up my bill now," I called to the owner, who was busy playing dice with a thin Furracian.

"Please find me a crow to take a message and a cart and driver worthy of the trip to Rome. If you are quick about it, I'll find you a little something extra for your trouble."

"I'll summon the crow but I fear that hiring a cart

is not possible Lord," spluttered the owner, choking on his rat kebab. "Tomorrow is the Caturnalia. Every cart and driver will be hired for the festival."

"Peus be praised!" called Eddipuss, with tears in his eyes. "All the other Gods be praised as well," he added. "I do not mean to leave any of you out!"

"Are you sure this is the right way to Rome?" I shouted over the clatter of the wheels. I instantly regretted it, for now Eddipuss began to talk about roads at great length. He moaned about the lot of the poor cart driver on the Ostia road. How the Emperor was only interested in his Golden House and his new canal. How he was letting the road fall to ruin. He didn't give off talking for a moment, not even to avoid the great grain carts as they carried the last of the harvest up the road to Rome. These titans were three times our size and nearly shook our tiny cart to pieces as they tore past us.

"I hope my luggage is tied down in the back," I shouted. "If one of my money pots came loose and fell off it would be a disaster."

"What's that?" called Eddipuss – struggling to hear me over the rattling ruts.

"Look out!" I hissed.

With an enormous crash, the world began to roll. Blow after blow slammed the light from my eyes. Although I felt every crash, I could hear nothing. I was lost to the world of sound as if buried under endless sand. At last, I felt claws at my back, heaving me out of the wreckage. Spluttering, I spat the dust from my mouth and shook myself thoroughly. As the morning sun burned my eyes, I thanked Mewpiter that I was still alive.

"Who's spilled this fellow's grain!" hissed a driver with a face a like a sick weasel. "He'll lose his job over this!"

Our cart had been turned over and was entirely covered in grain. My first thought was for the poor driver – and then for my own gold.

"Help! Do something! I am ruined!" I screamed in alarm. On hearing this Eddipuss sprang over to the crowd. A number of grain carts had stopped to help dig out their fellow driver.

"What fool is in charge of this rig? He should have had his eyes on the road!" spat the weasel-faced fellow.

"I was scratching a flea. I don't have eyes in the back of my head!" hissed Eddipuss, leaping onto a cart wheel. "Now listen all of you. Dig like dogs, for this citizen has two great pots of gold buried down there. Do as I say and you'll be rewarded!"

I was not exactly pleased to hear Eddipuss boasting of my riches, but perhaps it was the only way to get the crowd to help. A few of them began to dig. But the grain driver was not about to give up.

"You must give way to the larger vehicle. That is the rule of the road," hissed the driver.

"Learn to drive!" spat Eddipuss in a rage. "Don't

they teach you anything in Fleagypt?"

Now, I winced to hear Eddipuss speak this name again. For the last time he'd said it, in the market, it had caused a row that ended with blood, claws and a number of escaped snakes. Sure enough he was to prove my undoing once again. For when they heard this insult, some of the drivers fell into a dreadful rage. No words I could say could calm them.

Luckily, one of their number, a large tabby, took charge. I guessed that he was high up amongst the drivers as they all fell back as he stalked up.

"Two pots of gold buried down there you say? Well friends, I have a simple solution. The grain drivers will help dig them out and in return they shall have one to keep for all of their trouble."

On hearing this, Eddipuss flew into a rage and began to tear at his own fur.

"Robbers! Crooks!" he hissed. "I'd rather bargain with Hades himself! I'd get a better deal. I'll dig this Roman's things from under your cursed grain with my own two paws rather than agree to that. "

But as he began to dig, more grain spilled out onto our cart.

If giving away one pot of gold was the price of saving two, then it was a bargain I had to accept. Howling about it would not help. A single pot contained more money than I had ever known in my entire lifetime – ten lifetimes even.

Soon it was agreed and every driver set about the

search for my buried gold. As the sun worked her way around the noon sky, they scooped the grain from the wreck and piled it up at the side of the road.

It was two hours before they found the first pot. Shortly after a fish lunch they broke for cream, and again for fish biscuits. I had nearly given up hope when at last – with a cry – the second pot was found.

The two pots were placed side by side and the tabby called me over.

"Your choice friend," he purred.

"It matters little," I replied, knowing that there were equal amounts of gold in each pot. "I choose the black one."

"In the sight of Amun, it is yours. Take it and go in peace, brother," said the tabby. Eddipuss let out a hiss.

The drivers made a great fuss of heaving the black pot onto our cart and tieing it with ropes, glaring at Eddi all the while. Luckily, Caesar his broken-backed chariot dog had now returned. She looked even more miserable than before. Eddipuss heaved on the reins and we set off.

"What a day of woe!" I moaned. "Will we reach Rome before nightfall?"

Eddipuss brought the cart to a screaming halt behind a thicket.

"Why are we stopping? For Peus' sake, must we have more delays?"

Eddipuss looked at me in amazement.

"We're stopping to look inside that pot of course," he said. "I don't trust those filthy Fleagyptians as far as I can throw them."

I was about to give Eddipuss some advice about getting on with strangers from other lands when he let out a terrible hiss. I sprang down from the cart and saw him shaking the pot. It was empty – save for a pile of sand and a half-dead frog.

Eddipuss leapt in horror.

"Aaaarrrgh!" I wailed.

"Have no fear! I'm not poisonous," croaked the creature in a weak voice.

"It's not that," I gasped, stunned to hear a frog speak.

"What then?" it said in a low voice.

"My gold – it's all gone!" I wailed. "I finally made my fortune but now it has been stolen from under my nose. Am I to return to Rome, no better than a begging stray?"

The frog made no answer – with a final croak it gave an enormous leap, in the direction of my cushion. Then it lay completely still.

Now, I have no love for pond dwelling creatures – they are the least popular pets in the Feline Empire. Except in the far north of the Land of the Kitons, where the tribes are keen on newts. It is even said that the chiefs keep them in their homes and race them in regular competition around circular tracks.

I could not watch this creature croak its last breath.

It had leaped dangerously close to my wife's cushion and I dared not risk another stain.

"Fetch water! Quickly! Or it will die!' I cried.

"Who cares if it dies? It'll be tasty on a skewer."

I grabbed a water skin and squeezed out the last drop. Revived by the cool water, the frog kicked its legs weakly.

"I am ruined," I moaned.

"Cheer up," said Eddipuss. "At least we're not at our last gasp like our little green friend. Pass the water will you?"

But Fortune had spun us another wrong one. Our water skins were empty – they'd been slashed open.

"That frog looks moist," said Eddipuss. "It might keep us going for a while."

He began to eye it, as if it was prey. Batting away a swarm of black flies. I thought out loud:

"A talking frog must be worth something," I said. On hearing this, Eddipuss leapt like a kitten.

"A gift! A gift from the gods! We must save this beautiful creature – it's worth its weight in gold!" he cried, setting it on the cushion and kissing it for joy.

"Not on there, I beg of you!" I cried, fearing another stain. But I did not fancy picking it up.

"It's no use Eddipuss," I sighed. Without water, that frog cannot live and nor can we, for that matter."

Then I saw a most disgusting sight.

"What in Peus name are you doing?" I asked.

"Drooling!" he cried. "Help me. Dribble long and

hard, as if Peus himself had commanded it! We must save this wondrous creature's life."

Try as I might, my mouth was so dry that I could not manage a single drop of dribble.

"Here," said Eddi – giving me a strip of meat. "Chew on this! Get your juices going."

I had to work at eating it, pushing the leathery morsel around my dry mouth.

"What meat is this?" I asked. "It's got flavour but it's as hard as stone."

"It's a letter. Left by a crow this morning. And if it can save the life of this precious creature, then we are blessed that Fortune has placed it in my paw!"

I gave a hiss and tore the letter from his grasp. The writing was close to unreadable but I recognised it instantly. It was from my son.

"I hope he is not asking for more gold," I muttered, "For he will not like the answer this time."

The letter said:

> Send lawyers, swords and money!
> Dad – get me out of this... S.O.S.

So there I lay, at a cross roads, trying to spit on a dying frog. Two paths were before me. The first was the rutted road to Rome, where my foolish son had got himself into who knows what kind of trouble. The other was a dusty track leading into the scrub where those thieving Fleagyptians, and I shall now use that word whether they like it or not – had all scuttled off. Not content with taking half of all that I own, they'd tricked me out of both pots of gold. My rage turned upon the one who'd led me to this.

"That letter was addressed to me! Why in Peus's name did you not deliver it?" I hissed.

Eddipuss slunk low to the ground – and he gave no answer. By his nature, he was eager to please, but now he lay crestfallen in the dirt.

"Where have they taken him?" I asked.

Eddipuss sniffed the letter and let out a sucking noise which he made when he was deep in thought or in the middle of a negotiation about price.

"It's Hades Row, by the smell of it," he moaned.

I shuddered and my tail began to flick.

"My son? In prison? What has he done?"

Eddipuss gave a long list of crimes that S.O.S. might have committed – from parking a cart in a senator's space to offending the Emperor. I feared the last was the most likely. Nero had passed a law making it a crime to leave the theatre during one of his performances, which went on for hours. It is said that a Purrmanian gave birth to a litter of five in the middle of his performance of 'The Siege of Tray.'

I shuddered to think of my son in jail.

"Is there any hope of release?" I sighed.

"Maybe," said Eddipuss. "But you'll need a whole heap of gold to buy him out of Hades Row."

I tore into the dust with my claws.

"It's Rome's Worst Prison," he added.

"Gold! I laughed. "That is easy then. At least it would be easy if we could make Crownus burn time's candle backwards! Two days ago I had plenty of gold. Pots of it! Now it will be prison for my son, or worse."

"Having an only son must be a terrible worry," said Eddipuss, trying to calm me but not doing a very good job. "Did you never think of having another? It is said that if you have an 'heir', it is a good idea to have a 'spare' just in case."

I let out a mew of despair.

"In case death takes the first," he explained. "Just a little piece of friendly advice, for next time."

On hearing this, I tore at the ground again.

"Stop! I beg you!" cried Eddipuss. "Think about this! Having a daughter is supposed to be worse."

I was weeping bitter floods of tears when I heard a croaking sound. The frog was hopping around on my cushion, as fit as a trained flea. It had made an amazing recovery.

"Have no fear! If it is gold you need, I can show you the way," it croaked in a cheery voice.

I wiped the tears from my eyes and gasped.

"By Amun's fleece, don't stop crying!" said the frog. "Your tears are precious."

THE PRISON DIARY OF S.O.S.

Day I

This is the diary of the Son of Spartapuss, known as 'The Lord of the Lyre', a brave traveller from the Land of the Kitons. Here I will record the terrible events that have come to pass and led me to this dread cage...

It's no good. Whatever Purris says, I can't write my diary in that old-fashioned style. Haireena, if you ever get to read this, I want you to go all weepy over me. I don't want to sound like my father.

Purris is the only friend I've got in here. I've asked him to help me with this diary – as I never learned to write too well. I spent too much time practicing the lyre, I guess. Not any more though – the Emperor has taken my lyre away from me.

Purris says I'm a tragedy on four paws. Not bad eh? I never thought I'd get in with Rome's arty types! He's an actor – or at least he used to be before he got thrown in here.

I must stop writing now as I can hear the old jailor padding down the corridor with our rations. Today it's 'mouse bite stew', whatever that is.

Day II

It turned out to be 'mouse bits' stew. And not all of the bits in it were mouse.

As cells go, this one is pretty bad. They call it a cell but it's more of a hole. There's dirt on the floor, and dirt on the walls. The dirt in the corner tastes the best. Don't flick your tail in disgust – Haireena, a cat must eat anything to survive in here. They don't call it 'Hades Row' for nothing.

I can't believe my bad fortune – thrown in here for 'disrespecting' the Emperor. I didn't do anything!

Haireena, I hope you'll forgive me. A midnight walk around the Golden House wasn't the ideal place for our first date. For one thing, Nero's palace is only half finished. There were tools and ropes and things lying about all over the place. You could have easily tripped over and broken one of your beautiful claws on a hammer. And the second reason? It is death to set paw in an Imperial palace without permission. Only, I didn't know that. They could put a sign on the gates or something. There's nobody to blame, except perhaps my father. If only he'd got us tickets for the chariots like I told him to.

I suppose that curiosity got the better of us. With all the stories about the Emperor: how he keeps trained rats with little silver shoes; about his baths full of rare fish, heated to different temperatures; how he goes eel fishing with a golden sock.

Well, I did exactly as the Capo had told me. I waited till after the procession had passed, and kept you busy till dark. I played you every song I know – twice. As the sun sank like a firestone, the two of us padded towards the east gates of the palace.

If anyone asked, we were going to pretend to be

carpet merchants, come to measure the hall for a lion skin rug. The Spraetorians never even challenged us and we padded casually inside. What we saw next, would have stopped the heart of Hercatules or any hero you can name.

A figure in a golden collar bounded over to us from the far corner of the hall and cried:

"What is this vision I see before me?"

It was the Emperor Nero himself! A huge cat came lumbering to his side, a Purrmanian by the look of him. That brute was three times my size, and Haireena, I'm said to be big for a Kiton warrior.

You threw yourself to the ground and rolled over. I don't roll over for any cat but as it was the Emperor, I decided I'd make an exception. Then he spoke to you:

"Do not bow! Get up and dance for me."

Then he told me to take up my lyre and play.

Now, Haireena, I have to admit that my paws froze on the strings, not knowing what I should play for the Emperor. This was the biggest performance of my life. Nero might even hire me, for he must need musicians. I imagined myself in front of the throne, with a golden lyre in my paws. A crowd were showering me with coins. I snapped out of it and began the best tune I know – *The March of the Mewids*.

Haireena, you began to dance. I picture it every night as I close my eyes. It was a dance of great beauty and it takes my mind off the fleas in this cell.

As you danced, the Emperor let out a hiss and then leapt up, as if to strike me. Then he snatched the instrument from my shaking paws and began to play a fast reel. I hate to admit it, but he is a pretty good player. He began to sing in a clear voice:

> Treasure's for a spending
> mice can go a squeaking
> money's for the lending
> if your roof is leaking

As this last line rang through the great hall, one thousand golden flowers fell from the sky. You gasped at the sight of this. I reckoned they'd been held in nets and released with a hidden switch or something.

"Faster!" laughed Nero, and he began to play in double time. With a sudden twang a string snapped.

"Shame!" called the great brute at his side.

"Fear not, Spitulus, I will finish the piece on three strings," said the Emperor.

I watched his paws as they walked around the lyre. They seemed to know where they were going. You began to dance again. Moments later, there was second twang.

"Hades Paws!" he called. "A hunk of driftwood, strung with slaves' guts would play better."

"Shall I call the slaves to fetch your golden lyre," asked a pale tabby at the Emperor's side. I'd hardly noticed him next to the immense bulk of the other.

"By Peus, I will not allow it!" hissed Nero – and he snatched up the lyre and began to play again on two strings. His paws raced around the fretboard.

"Surely, you cannot play the piece with just one string?" cried the tabby. "Why Purrcury himself could not play that tune on just one string!"

I remember that you gasped in awe Haireena.

"Nonsense!" said the Emperor – and he took up the tune again, his paws dancing on the frets.

The great brute began to cheer and clap. I didn't know whether to join in or not. I knew Nero had snapped my strings on purpose. It was a trick to impress the crowd – but I had to admire his skill.

"What did you think female?" asked the Emperor, when his song was finished. "Was my tune more to your liking than that Kiton's grim march?"

Haireena, you said nothing. Up lumbered the big one. Did I call him a brute before? I was right!

"Speak without fear although your life depends on it. Who played best, the ginger one or your Emperor?"

You gazed up at the hulk:

"Haven't I seen you on a poster?" you asked.

"Perhaps, at the arena," he replied. "But be quick and answer the Emperor's question!"

"The Emperor is the best of course. His singing is far sweeter than the wailing of the ginger."

I forgive you for saying that to save your life.

"Excellent," laughed Spitulus.

"You are a good judge female. There are few well-trained ears in this land, so yours shall stay attached to your lovely head."

Spitulus and Purris laughed uneasily. Haireena, you began to cry.

"Hold!' cried the Emperor. "Look! I've moved her to tears. She's a beautiful crier. What eyes – like Queen Cleocatra herself!"

You stood frozen, and you could not answer.

"No, Caesar. Not Cleocatra, I think," said Spitulus. "More like Queen Kandmeet. This beauty is from the ancient Kingdom of the Kushionites, if I am not mistaken."

The lumbering brute was quite well-spoken.

"Speak Queen! Is Spitulus right?"

"Yes Lord, I am from that land," you answered.

The Emperor gazed at the painted stars on his golden ceiling.

"From the Land of the Kushionites? This is a pawtent. A sign from the Gods."

He strummed a sad chord on my lyre. Then he drew close to you – within a whisker's length, and whispered:

"You pretty, will go with Spitulus here."

"No Best and Greatest," said the hulk. "It is too dangerous."

"I insist on it," said the Emperor. "The gods will it. Go female, you belong to him now. Have no fear – for they call him 'The Educated Gladiator'"

And with that, the Emperor bounded off with you and the others at his tail.

Perhaps I should have been happy that he didn't want my head on a spike, but my heart was broken. Without a second thought I called out:

"Wait! Emperor! Wait!"

The Emperor stopped in his tracks.

"Did something squeak? Did I hear a mouse in my golden house?" he laughed. Padding softly towards me, he fixed me with a stare.

"I hope it was a mouse. For it is death to speak to a god without their permission! Spitulus! Tear off his tail and feed it to my new hounds!"

The giant seemed sad as he sprang towards me. He had great big claws like dinner knives.

You gasped Haireena. I remember thinking: 'This is it!'

I wanted to die well because you were watching.

As the brute raised his paw to strike, I said a silent prayer and got ready for Summerlands, or whatever the next world has in store for me.

Then, dear Haireena, you let out a wail and put your paws in front of your pretty eyes.

"Hold!" cried the Emperor. "I do not want to stain my new mosiac. There is enough red in it already. What would you ask of me? Squeak up?"

"Excuse me great Emperor," I said, staring at the ruler of the known world. "Can I have my lyre back?"

AUGUSTPUSS X
August 10th

As I stood weeping over a half dead frog, I could think of nothing but my foolish son – and how we could get him out of Rome's worst prison without so much as a bronze coin for the jailor's paw. We trudged through the hot scrub country in the hills near Ostia and my front paws were playing me up again. As the sun slowly dipped, at least one of our party was feeling better.

"My friends, our worries are over!" said Jebel. "My mistress has treasure. Return me to her and you will be rewarded."

"Your mistress?" laughed Eddi. "Didn't she sell pots at the market in Ostia?"

"The pot seller is not my mistress," croaked Jebel.

"Where can we find her?" I asked wearily.

"Tonight, the light of Amun's fire will lead us to her."

"This treasure," said Eddipuss in excitement. "Does your mistress keep it in an ancient tomb? Or in a secret treasure room? Or in a magic chest or some such place?"

"No," said the frog. "She keeps it underground."

I'd heard enough of this nonsense. Wearily, I got up and began to strike camp.

"Oooooh!" I cried. My pads were red raw.

"Where are you going?" called Eddi.

"I must get after the robbers. If I cannot find them, then I must run to Rome and plead with my son's jailors."

"That's pleading useless," said Eddi. "Without gold, that son of yours is stuck in Hades Row, unless…"

He sniffed the air and his expression changed.

"Unless what?" I hissed impatiently.

"Unless the frog is right. Maybe his Mistress is rich? I know that everything I've said so far has turned out to be wrong. But hear me now. That treasure exists."

"The heat's turned your head," I hissed. "I'll show you treasure. There are two pots of gold already out there that belong to me. We must find the robbers and get them back somehow!"

I popped Jebel into the pot, grabbed the cushion and sprang away down the track.

A chill wind got up that night, and so we rested in the shade of a wild olive grove.

"Our cause is lost," I moaned. "We are ten hours at least behind the robbers."

"Three hours, not ten," croaked Jebel.

"I didn't know frogs could tell the time," hissed Eddipuss. "How do you work that out?"

"They'll be running, not riding," answered the frog. They are closer than you think."

I looked at the creature in amazement. It was strange to hear such wisdom from a frog with an extremely small head.

The philosopher Sprayo thinks that a part of our soul lives in our heads. The bigger a creature's head, the bigger his brain must be. However, I myself have always doubted this theory. For there is a tribe in the east of the Land of the Kitons who are known to have unusually large heads and they are also said to be one of the stupidest of tribes. Their king once sat on the beach and commanded the waves not to come in. Nobody knows why he did this. I expect he'd spent many hours building an interesting 'stonecastle' or something.

At any rate, at last we had a lucky spin from Fortune's wheel. We came across an abandoned farm that stood on a small round hill. The farmyard had a well in it. Jebel leaped for joy at the smell of the water and we only just stopped him from diving into it.

As dawn rose the puddle grey skies turned lighter. Then we saw a flash of dazzling blue sea on the horizon.

"The port! cried Eddipuss, "I bet they're planning to escape by sea. We might still be in time to stop them if we're quick."

"Unless they are already gone!" I moaned.

There were three ships leaving the port. One of them had my gold in its hold, most likely. I began to wail:

"It's too late! We've lost the robbers. Unless we get my gold back, I fear it will be blood and sandals in the arena for my poor son."

THE SECRET DIARY OF S.O.S.

Day III

If only you could see me writing these words Haireena. You'd see that my pen shakes in my paw as I tell the next part of this tale. Ha! Well it would if I was a scardicat – but they drag you up tough in the Land of the Kitons.

Today, I gave the last thing I owned – a flea comb – to a guard who says he can get my message out by crow. I've said a prayer to Paws. He's the god of war, but I think father once said that he also does guards – right? If the mighty Paws wills it, the guard will be as good as his word, and the crow will bring this letter to my father. I pray it will fly straight because I can't stand it in here.

Lord Paws – hear my promise. I vow now that I'll catch up with the brute who stole Haireena away from me. Whatever his mission is, it will be his last!

Day IV

News of hope! There's a rumour going around that tomorrow, we prisoners are to be released. It is the Caturnalia festival and the Emperor is giving out pardons. Can you believe it? I can't wait to tell Purris – who is in the cell opposite.

Day V

Dread news! Purris says that we are to be released

– into a school for gladiators. The Emperor is picking prisoners for the Games at the Carturnalia and fifty more fighters are needed. I told Purris not to worry – the gladiators is fixed – like the chariots back in my homeland. They bribe the dogs or the drivers it is said.

Day VI

The cell next to mine is empty – and so it looks like Purris and I are going to be next. Purris says our only hope is to look too sick or too weak to make an entertaining fight. This is a problem for us gingers with our thick fur. We look bigger, so we get picked first. Beneath this fur, I'm a bag of bones. Haireena – will you spray a little prayer for me, on that alter of yours?

Day VII

The cats on the corridor are all talking about the games. Apparently, someone has given the Emperor a present of sixty cat-eating hounds in cages! Probably some savage chief from Maul, trying to impress him.

Lord Paws – another word in your mighty ear. When I prayed that you'd get me in to the festival, I didn't mean as a gladiator or as bait for a hound!

Day VIII

Half of Hades Row is gone now. Purris has persuaded me to shave my fur off in order to make myself look less like a gladiator. Haireena – I hope you like the short furred look. Purris says it makes me look a bit less warlike.

Day XI

Is there no glue to be had in all of Rome? I was half way through shaving, when I heard the very worst news. Those who are not picked as gladiators are going to be used to train the Emperor's sixty cat-eating hounds! I heard that the beasts will not come out of their cages, unless they have live prey to chase.

Haireena – this is goodbye. They're coming for us next. Please remember your poor S.O.S!

Day X

Well Haireena, I'm not yet a gladiator, beast fodder or bait for the cat-eating hounds of Maul. You won't believe where they've taken me. I am writing my diary from inside the Emperor's Golden House. Yes! I was wrong to curse the unfinished palace, for it's saved my hide.

They need more work gangs to finish it off. When they saw that Purris and I were shaved, they mistook us for stone masons from Fleagypt. Purris says that in Fleagypt, the Furroah always shaves his slaves. Apparently, he doesn't want them moulting all over his final resting place and carrying hairs through into the afterlife. What a lucky mistake for us!

Today we started work on a new fish pool for the Emperor. Purris has great control of his chisel.

I'm learning fast but I accidently chipped the fin off a leaping carp near the Imperial plughole. I hope the Master Mason doesn't see it. He's in charge here and he's always stalking around criticising our work.

Day XI

Today the Master Mason noticed the chipped carp and gave me a terrible roasting about it. He's got hold of a cat-eating hound.

"It needs feeding, and it likes gingers," he hissed. "Those waves look like a dog's dinner. Sort it out, or you'll be a hound's breakfast."

Day XII

I've been very careful with my chisel – so the Master's cat-eating hound will go hungry. Purris, who is good at this artistic stuff, has got me doing waves. "They're a safer bet than leaping carp," he says.

Day XIII

As he made his inspection today, the Master Mason was impressed with Purris's work. He even tried to shake paws with him in a funny way.

The Master did not single me out today because when he came to my part of the line, there was a dreadful barking. He had to spring off to sort it out.

Day XIV

My waves are rolling on nicely. I'm starting to

think that I have a knack for this. I might even become a Grand Carver, one day. Purris is not so sure that I'd make Grand Carver but he says with a lot of effort and six or seven years of training, I might make the rank of 'Little Chipper'.

Day XV

Disaster! I've cracked the rim of the Emperor's bath. It was not my fault – my chisel jumped out of my paw. I was distracted by a giant bee from one of the Emperor's private hives. I tried to put right my mistake with a bit of crafty carving – but my chisel slipped for the second time. Now Neptune only has two prongs on his trident. I hope the Master doesn't spot it.

Day XVI

Haireena, listen my love. Purris says that the Master Mason is bound to find out about the two pronged trident. The whole camp is laughing about it. I must make a run for it this very night. These may be the last words that I write to you. Pray to whatever gods you have in the Land of the Kushionites that I 'll come safely through this.

Day XVII

Fair Haireena, You must be wondering what happened. I've escaped, but soon I'll face another danger. There is just time to write these lines before I must be on the move again. Sit down on one of the famous cushions from your homeland and get comfortable, for the tale is long.

As you know, I could not stay here with the Master sniffing around. So I waited till all were asleep, and took up my chisel, which I had secretly 'borrowed' from work. I placed it on the chain around my paw. I had no hammer, so I took up a great stone block instead. Just as I was about to strike a blow, a voice at my side cried:

"By Vulcan's beak! What are you doing?"

"What do you think?" I called back. "Be silent unless you want a mouth full of stone."

"Not like that! You'll blunt your chisel. It's made for chipping stone, not cutting chains. Call yourself a stone mason? Go back to sleep, before you wake the Master."

I had no choice but to give up.

Later that night, there was a terrible racket. Horrible growling and shouts came from nearby. Taking my chance, I began to hammer madly at the chain where it met the post. After five blows, the chain came out of its fixing, lock and all. I heaved it over my shoulder and ran to find Purris but there was no sign of him.

The Golden House is vast so I didn't know which way to run. We masons were camping outside the Emperor's apartments. I decided to head for the garden walls and put as much distance between me and that howling as possible.

There was an enormous moon – which we call Churn's moon in The Land of the Kitons, after Churn The Hunter. It was easy for me to see in the dark and I'd almost made it to the wall when I heard a noise behind me. Padding through the flower beds, I caught the scent of a creature. Then I trod in something horrible. It seems that the Imperial Gardeners had put something down on the roses to make them grow better.

At last I made it to the wall. It was ten tails high Haireena, but I scaled it in a single bound, or maybe two. Anyway, my heart was flapping like a pheasant as I sat on top of the wall. Then I caught sight of something crouching in the shadows. Taking no chances, I decided to pounce.

It went down quicker than fish on a feast day. I had my claw at its throat and was about to strike it with my chain – just to be on the safe side, when I heard a squeaking voice:

"In the name of Peus! Don't you recognise me?"

"Purris!" I cried. "What are you doing here?"

"Searching for a way out," he gasped, still winded from my attack.

"And it looks like you've found one. Well – thanks for looking after your friend. You don't even need to escape. You're the favourite of the Master Mason. I can't believe you would run off and leave me. There's a word for that, where I come from: 'turntail!'"

And with that I rolled to my feet and sprang off.

"Wait!" he hissed. "Come back."

"Forget it," I hissed back.

A terrible howl tore through the night.

"For Peus' sake! What was that?" I asked.

"What do you think!" hissed Purris. "It's the Master Mason's cat-eating hound."

"Have no fear," I told him. "It's on the other side of that wall. We are free!"

"You are wrong on both counts," moaned Purris. "Now flee!"

He was right. We hadn't escaped to the countryside. We were still inside the grounds of the Golden House. Nero's palace is bigger than the largest of our towns at home and we'd only got as far as the Emperor's fish farm. Purris says he has a hundred fish pools, stocked with fish from both river and sea.

We ran until our pads ached.

"Wait!" I called, for Purris looked a bit tired. "We must rest for a while." Purris stopped in his tracks.

"I'm fine to go on, but you look the worse for wear," he said.

I was still carrying the iron chain. We Kitons are no complainers, but it was difficult to run with that on your back. When Purris saw it, he gasped.

"I see the Master still has his claws in you," he said. "You must get that off, or we'll never float out of here."

"Why didn't I think of that." I said. "I'll just gnaw my leg off and then the chain will slip off easily."

"Don't take that tone," said Purris in a wounded voice. "Or I won't let you use this."

A small silver key glinted in the light of the hunter's moon.

"I stole it from the Master Mason this morning," laughed Purris. "I was going to come back for you, as soon as I'd found the way out."

Well Haireena, I could have kissed him. As he's an actor, I expect he does a fair bit of kissing – down at the amphitheatre.

As he unlocked the chain, I decided to say a few words of thanks:

"Look, Purris. You've been a good friend to me. I am sorry…" I began.

But before I could get the words out there was a terrible snarling and an enormous black hound bounded out of the shadows. It was twice the size of the largest chariot dog at home. It looked annoyed – as if it had applied for a job at the pits of Hades, but it'd had to settle for guarding the Emperor's fish pools instead.

We froze, silent as standing stones while the beast leered at us, its red tongue lolling around its mouth, like they do.

"A cat-eating hound!" cried Purris in terror.

I looked the foul creature in the reds of its eyes.

"It looks like they sorted out the problem of how to get them to come out of their cages," I said.

"Show no fear!" said Purris, but he was shaking as

he spoke.

"That's right!" I said. "Act like prey, and you will be eaten like prey."

This beast was bred by the very worst barbarians of Maul and hand fed with special meat that... Er, I dare not write what sort of meat they feed them with as I may upset you Haireena.

It came closer and showed its teeth. The front ones had been filed into dagger sharp points by its trainer. Its breath reeked. If any hound trainers ever get to read this diary, I'd suggest a little less filing and a little more brushing – if you know what I mean. Or why not train them to do it themselves and leave some fang brushes in their cages?

The horrid hound stood and stared.

"Why isn't it trying to eat us?" I asked.

"It doesn't know what to do," said Purris. "Maybe its because we've stood our ground. Cat Eating Hounds are not bred for their intelligence."

"We can't stay here all day!" I replied. "When I say the word, get ready to leap for it."

"Have your lost your reason?" cried Purris. "If we run, we're dead meat."

"See those statues," I explained. "You go to Mewpiter, I will go to Caturn. It cannot follow us all the way up there."

The beast let out a rumbling growl.

"But Mewpiter is further away," whined Purris.

"Yes – but Caturn is the harder climb. Do you

fancy getting a grip on his sickle? If you want to risk the reaper then that's fine, we'll swap."

"Alright," called Purris.

It was a long leap to the statues which stood at each end of a high wall. The sides of the wall were smooth marble – but there was a vine where you could get a claw in. Taken at a run, we might make it.

The hound growled, as if it knew what we were planning.

"Now!" hissed Purris and he shot towards his statue like a bullet from a sling. The great hound tore after him. I've never seen anything that big and ugly move so fast – apart from the time the barbarians visited the biscuit sale in our village.

Well Haireena, I took my chance and sprang towards the other statue. I had one claw on the base of the wall when I heard a cry. Looking back, I saw that the hound had Purris cornered.

I let out my worst hiss to get its attention. I'm a good hisser, Haireena, but this hound was cunning. It didn't want to leave Purris in order to chase me. Spotting a loose stone in the wall, I hurled it at the demon dog.

"Aaaargh!" came a scream. I'd hit Purris on the nose.

"For Peus sake! Are you trying to kill me?" he howled.

The creature was distracted for a moment and Purris took his chance and he was soon safe on top of the wall. I scaled it with ease and we sat laughing at the foolish beast below us.

"We are saved!" cried Purris, jumping for joy. Sitting on top of the statues, we had an eagle's view of the grounds. I was surprised to see a long, thin stretch of water.

"Is that a fish pond?" I asked. "It's very long."

"That's a canal, you fool!" cried Purris.

"A what?" I asked. For we don't have such things in the land of the Kitons.

"It's like a river – that's been dug out. I heard that the Emperor was having one put in. It'll take us all the way to the Port of Ostia.

"I'm not going to Ostia!" I said. "I cannot leave Rome. I must find Haireena."

Yes – dearest. Even then I was thinking of you.

"I have news for you," said Purris. "The Emperor has sent Spitulus on a mission to find the source of the Nile."

Well Haireena, I could have kissed him again.

"That is the best news," I called. "Paws and all the others be praised! We'll go there this very night!"

Purris laughed.

"You do know about the source of the Nile, don't you?"

"Obviously," I replied.

"The quest will lead you through many wild places," said Purris.

"Fine," I nodded. I was sure that The Source of the

Nile fish restaurant could be found on the east side – probably somewhere near the Fatted Carp.

"Lead on friend!" I called.

In my homeland I didn't pay much attention at school, except in music where I was naturally at the top of the class. Only Strumpuss got a higher mark – but he had a private tutor to help him. I wished I'd studied harder. For the source of the Nile is not a fish restaurant on the east side of the city, as I found out.

Purris led me to the bank of the canal and leapt neatly into a barrel.

"We can paddle our way out in these," he said.

"There's one problem with that. I can't swim."

Purris flicked his tail. He looked disappointed.

"What do you mean, you can't swim?" he asked.

"We're not big swimmers in the Land of the Kitons," I said. Our rivers are cold and they've got crabs and flies on the bottom. Not to mention the leeches.

"Never mind," he said. "You walk if you want – I'll float in this barrel. Keep a look out for guards. It is nearly dawn and they'll be changing shift."

We padded on through the early dawn and hid through the day. It was all going well, as if the gods were smiling on our journey. But a terrible thing was about to happen. It is the saddest thing that I have had to write so far Haireena, so forgive me if you do not like sad tales.

"This is the last lock," said Purris. "We'll join up

with the river that flows down to the port. Then we can float downstream and find you a ship..."

He was interrupted by a challenge.

"WHO GOES THERE?"

"Release the rope and pull the lever!" said Purris.

Water began to bubble in, filling the lock.

"Quickly!" cried Purris. "Are you trying to drown me? You'll flood it if you don't open the gates."

As I tried to work out what to do, Purris leapt from the barrel.

"Help me up!" he cried. The sides were steep. I reached out to pull him up but I slipped on the wet planks. I felt the sting of the cold water. The lock was filling up fast.

"Help!" I cried, thrashing around in the water.

"Climb inside the barrel!" cried Purris. "Get in quickly while I open the gate."

Somehow I managed to get inside. There was too much water – the lock was overflowing.

"Take this!" called Purris – throwing me the lid. "Hold on for your life, or learn to swim!"

I pulled the lid down onto the barrel. It was as dark as a long barrow.

"STOP! IN THE NAME OF THE EMPEROR!" hissed a voice.

The wood squeaked with the force of the water. I could feel the water pressing me against the gate. The old timber began to buckle. At last, the lock gates burst open.

AUGUSTPUSS XIII
August 13th

The Lepida

I stood on the quayside nursing my aching pads and looking out at the stone grey sea. Had my gold sailed off already? Or was it aboard one of the last ships still moored in the port of Ostia?

I'd learned that it was two weeks to what is called the 'closed sea'. Few ships would dare to set sail now.

With aching pads, I slunk back down the dock road to see if Eddipuss had discovered anything. As we made our way to the meeting place, Jebel asked a question.

"How can you close the sea? Your Emperor is powerful – not even my mistress could do that."

"They don't really close it." I replied. "It's just the name for the time of storms. To sail in the season of gales and fog means shipwreck and probable death."

Just then, Eddipuss arrived.

"Aye aye shipmates!" he called.

AUGUSTPUSS XIV
August 14th

The *Lepida* is not exactly a wild cat of the seas. But it lives up to its name because every fish biscuit aboard is covered in small black spots. We set sail two days ago. I cannot blame Eddipuss for getting us on board such a wretched wreck. We had no money to buy our passage, so it follows that we must work our passage. If my gold is not aboard this ship, perhaps we can catch up with the robbers in the east? Failing that, we must seek the frog's mistress and claim a reward.

With heavy hearts, we padded up the gang plank. I clung onto my pot and my cushion, whilst Eddipuss carried Jebel in a bucket. At the top of the plank, crouched an aged sea cat – as gnarled as a hunk of driftwood.

"Aye, aye! Can we come aboard Captain?" said Eddipuss, a little too heartily for my liking.

"MATE!" corrected the shadow.

"Thanks mate. Hey Spartapuss – looks like we'll be amongst friends on this voyage."

"I'm THE MATE, not YOUR MATE you stupid squab!" growled the old sailor.

"Excuse my friend. Could you show us to our cabins please?" I asked.

"CABINS?" hissed the Mate, swinging his head round and pointing an ear towards me.

He sprang down the plank and began to sniff at us suspiciously. Then he padded up to the bucket, which contained Jebel, and began to paw at it. I'd warned the frog to keep completely silent, as sailors are a most superstitious lot.

"By Neptune's pointed stick! What's that you've

got there?"

"That's just an ingredient," said Eddipuss. "We're famous cooks from the land of Maul. We use all sorts of funny ingredients in our dishes, from foreign parts mostly."

The mate sniffed at the bucket for a long time and finally he gave a cough.

"Smells like a frog. Throw it overboard. The Captain hates frogs," he hissed.

"Help!" cried Jebel, from within the bucket.

I tried to cover his cry with a coughing fit.

"The frog isn't for eating," said Eddipuss. "We wouldn't serve you frog. We're using him to make 'frog water'. The water that the frog has been sitting in all day. It's the best thing for boiling udders with."

I looked at Eddipuss in amazement, not knowing where he was headed with this.

"He's right," I said, "It's a dish fit for the Emperor himself. Once you've tasted our boiled cow's udders in frog water, you'll never forget them."

"He should know," said Eddi. "He's from the land of the Kitons. They do a lot of boiling over there. They are masters of the caldron, you know."

The Mate's amber eyes flashed and he began to bristle.

"Get up here!" he growled.

When we were aboard, he ordered us to haul in the gang plank. Then he called to the harbour crew to untie the ropes that held us to the dock.

"Haul in the lines!" he ordered.

Eddi stood for a moment, wondering what to do.

"By Hades' fetid pits! Haul in the lines. Get a shift on!"

The Mate picked up a rope, coiled it in a flash and practically threw it at Eddipuss. Eddi jumped clear as the rope slammed into the deck. Then the Mate stuck out a paw in my direction and jabbed the air with his claws.

"COOKS? COOKS! Two of you. You'll do more than cook to earn your passage on this ship."

Before we could protest he grabbed a couple of buckets and set us to work 'scraping the decks' as the sailors call it.

As we took to the open sea, our little ship began to roll wildly and I was thrown about the deck. The Mate soon set us to work, growling out orders.

I was surprised to see that Eddipuss was in his element with ropes and knots, and he stood steady on the deck despite the battering waves.

That night, the sea was black as squid ink and a hollow wind chilled us from nose to tail. In the galley, we ate in silence. I was too tired to speak. My front paws stung and I had to will my eyes to stay open.

I woke with a start to find that the miserable Mate had joined us and sat licking at a bowl of Eddi's stew.

"Not bad is it? Can you taste the frog water?" asked Eddipuss, forgetting that this was the same fellow who had thrown a rope at him.

The Mate stared into his stew.

With no one but me to talk to, Eddipuss had been silent for hours. Now he was babbling like a brook. I wished someone could put a dam in him before he talked us into more trouble.

"Why is this ship so short of crew?" he asked.

"Why do you think?" growled the Mate.

It was the sort of question that does not need an answer. But Eddipuss answered it anyway.

"I think, it's because you're sailing at the wrong time," offered Eddipuss. "I've heard that it is madness to try to cross to Fleagypt in a boat so small at the time of storms."

The Mate didn't answer. He just stared at his bowl as if he could burn holes in the pewter with his glazed eyes.

"Or maybe its because of the Captain," continued Eddipuss. "They say..."

The Mate let out a hiss and dashed his bowl to the deck.

"What ABOUT the Captain?" he hissed.

He shot Eddipuss a dark look – as if he was about to tear his throat out.

Poor Eddipuss began to shake uncontrollably.

"He's very sorry. He meant no offence," I gasped.

"Answer me squab!" demanded the Mate.

"Something about him being mad?" said Eddi.

I threw poor Eddipuss a line.

"We are all mad," I laughed. "Mad to sail so near the closed sea. If I had a coin for every time I heard that, I wouldn't need to go on a treasure hunt."

I slopped out another bowl of flatfish stew.

"Take this to the Captain now Eddipuss. Be quick before for it grows cold."

"Give it here, I'll see to that," hissed the Mate. "Get back to your duties."

When he'd gone, Eddipuss and I agreed that something was not right about the Mate. He had something to hide – but was it my stolen gold?

"I beg you, take every chance you can to look for it," I whispered. "Leave no scent unsniffed, for my son's life depends upon it."

"Don't worry," said Eddipuss. "If your gold is aboard this ship, we'll find it."

AUGUSTPUSS XV

August 15th

I've been on a few strange ships in my time but none stranger than *The Lepida*.

For one thing, we had neither sight or sniff of the Captain. It seems that Eddipuss and I are the only crew, apart from the 'Mad Mate' – as Eddi now calls him. I am never one for name calling but his behaviour is getting stranger and stranger. Today he ran to the side and sprang up onto the rail, sticking his nose into the air. Then he called for Eddipuss to join him up there. Eddi sprang up next to him and the two of them perched like a couple of seagulls on a rubbish ditch, staring out into the blue.

The wind was howling, so I had no clue what was said. Later, I asked Eddi what had happened

"It was very strange," said Eddi, throwing dead flies into Jebel's bucket. The frog was miserable now that he had to stay in the galley all day so Eddi had taken to feeding him bluebottles to cheer him up.

"What were you doing? You could have been blown overboard."

"He ordered me up there," said Eddi. "So I couldn't say 'No'. He sniffed at the air and started shouting: 'I smell a ship!' Then he got me to look over the yard-arm and tell him what I could see.

'Nothing!' I told him.

'Look harder squab!' he growled. I strained my eyes and saw a spot on the horizon, the size of an ant.

'A ship!' I cried.

'I knew it!' he hissed. 'What's her heading?'

'I can't tell,' I said. 'I can only just see a tiny speck with red sails.'

I feared he was going to throw me to the sharks. But instead he thanked me.

'Well done Squab. You cook like a lug but you've got eyes like a gull,'" he said.

"What happened then?" I asked.

"He took me to the tiller and told me to steer towards the red ship."

AUGSTPUSS XVI

August 16th

We have now searched the ship but there is not a sniff of my gold.

The last place I looked was in the Captain's cabin. I crept to the door and pushed at it, expecting it to be locked but it swung wide open. There is nothing in there but charts and papers. I left in a hurry, fearing what the Mate might do if he found me in that place. He is as gruff with me as ever. He gave me a roasting this morning for moving one of his buckets.

"Everything on this ship has its proper place. Don't put a paw on anything unless I tell you," he growled.

He has no love for Jebel either. Last night I caught him sniffing at the frog's bucket – and making a most peculiar face.

But if the frog and I are equally hated, the Mate has taken an unusual liking to Eddipuss. The two of them have worked together all day. He often tells Eddipuss to take the tiller and set our course.

As you know, I am no great climber so I try to stay on deck. I still do not yet have my 'sea paws'.

I've been stuck here in the galley, with just a frog to talk to. Even Jebel was silent. I do not think the sea air agrees with him.

AUGUSTPUSS XVII

August 17th

We are chasing the ship with the red sails. Eddipuss says it may be bound for the land of Fleagypt. I must have another word with him about using such a rude name for that country, as it will lead us into more trouble. I have no clue why the Mate should want to chase that ship. Is it some superstition of the sailors that they do not like red sails?

Eddipuss was most excited about the chase.

"By Fleanus' Fluffy Ruff!" he cried. He is becoming quite the sailor and picking up a lot of these sayings. "We'll stick to that ship like a limpet to a rock. If fortune wills it, we'll make port in Fleagypt and catch up with the filth who stole your gold."

"That's a fair lot of fortune we'll be needing," I sighed. I thought of my poor son and the treasure we'd need to buy him out of Hades Row.

Eddipuss sat completely still, then gave a wobble as if he was making ready to spring. He'd spotted a fat bluebottle which would make a tasty treat for Jebel. He sprang at the fly, swiping at it with both paws. I wished Eddi would stop chasing insects – for they can sting or bite. I tried to distract him with talk.

"The Furroahs know how to treat robbers."

"They do indeed!" cried Eddipuss. "Oh yes!" he cried, warming to one of his favourite topics. "I'll say that for the Fleagyptians. They know what to do with robbers. First they take their claws out, one by one, so they can't scratch. And then they pull their back teeth out, so they can't bite. And then they chop their..."

Eddipuss continued like this for some time until I began to feel sick. I suppose it made a change to feel something other than sea sickness.

"Enough!" I hissed, when my stomach could take no more. "It'd serve them right for stealing my gold."

"Aye!" hissed Eddipuss. "And you'll not believe what they do to grave robbers, it's ten times worse."

"Grave robbers?" I asked.

"Yes, in Fleagypt. It is a disgusting land. For who would want to break into a tomb and steal some old bones? Peus alone knows how they cook them. It is a terrible problem out there, it is said."

At last Eddi caught the fly and flicked it into the frog's bucket.

"Grave robbers are not after bones!" I laughed. "When one of the great Furroahs, the rulers of that land dies, he buries all his treasure with him, in a great triangle shaped tomb called a Purramid. That's where..."

Before I could finish, Eddipuss let out a frightened mew.

"What's wrong?" I asked.

Eddi crouched over Jebel's bucket, fishing around frantically with his paws

"It's the poor little frog," he said slowly. "He's as dead as a nail."

THE SECRET DIARY OF S.O.S.

Day XX

Haireena my dear, I am still writing this diary for you. One day I hope to place it in your paw. You have such pretty paws. Not like those Roman females with their painted claws. Or the 'she–warriors' of our tribe with their great paws like battle-axes!

How am I? Fine, thank you for asking. But I'm afraid that this ship stinks! The food on board is worse than it was in prison, and the waves never stop. Never mind ordering the tide not to come in, someone needs to order it to stop going up and down!

Haireena you are probably wondering how I got onto this ship. Well, I cannot say exactly – but I guess that when Purris opened the lock gates, my barrel must have floated all the way down to the docks. Then I was loaded onto this ship, mistaken for a barrel of lickamen sauce.

It wasn't easy Haireena, being stuck in the dark for days. I only survived by scraping the bottom of the barrel.

Not everyone likes to dip their food in rotten fish sauce. I hope you love licakmen Haireena – as it is impossible to get the fishy smell out of my coat. Perhaps it was a bad batch of sauce, made from fish that had gone off before it rotted?

What happened to Purris? I do hope he escaped. I wanted to go back and help but the lid of my barrel was on so tight, I couldn't shift it, though I pushed with all my strength. Which is a lot Haireena. But it wasn't enough and I had to wait till someone broke it open.

I feared that I would die there and rot into the rest of the sauce. But at last, one day I saw the light again and fell out into a smelly wooden box. The box turned out to be the galley of a ship and the smell was coming from me.

Misis, the cook's daughter, has been so kind. If it wasn't for her, I'd have been taken for a stowaway and thrown to the sharks. She's hidden me in the hold of the galley and she gives me treats.

Have no fear Haireena – when we reach port I'll slip away and find out where they have taken you. Until then I'll live on my wits. No one will find me here!

Day XXI

What's that banging? Someone has found me!

Day XXII

Luckily, it was only Misis' father. He's a grizzled cook with a rack of nasty looking choppers. Misis gave me away. She's got rather an annoying laugh. Her father didn't look too pleased to see me. It could easily have come to claws but Misis started to cry and he changed his mind.

"Well, 'Son of Spartapuss' is it eh?" he hissed.

"With that ginger coat you'll stick out like a donkey at the camel club. You'll have to stay below decks, or it'll be the dog of nine tails for us both."

"My thanks," I replied. "Do the dogs really have nine tails in your land? That's a sight I'd like to see."

"You won't like this one," he growled. "It bites!" Then he showed me his back. It was covered in scars. The fur was matted and falling out in patches. He laughed, and threw me a few scraps.

"Thanks," I said, tearing into the dry meat as if it was the finest dormouse. "I won't be any trouble."

"You are trouble already!" he said.

We heard the pad of iron-shod paws coming down the corridor. Misis opened the door of the hold.

"Quickly!" she begged. "You must hide!"

The door slammed behind me as I jumped into the darkness.

Day XXIII

Haireena, I'm sick of being shut up down here. I'm not sure that I trust the old cook. Anyone with scars that bad must be a criminal.

Day XXIV

My father is always telling me to "look for the good in everyone you meet." But my mother knows what she's talking about. She is one of the most suspicious cats in our whole tribe.

"Trust no one!" she says, "Especially at family events like weddings and funerals."

As I crouched in the damp of the hold, I began to wonder what that old cook was up to. I've gnawed a hole in the door. Now I'll be able to spy on them when they shut me up tonight.

Day XXV

Haireena, I have changed my plan. I have decided to get back into my barrel and float to freedom. Lickamen sauce is not that bad. Besides, I've got a strange feeling that something bad is about to happen.

Last night, I waited until shut up time, as usual.

"Please!" hissed Misis, opening the door to the hold. "You must hide quickly!"

Looking through a crack in the door, I could see about half of the galley. My eyes wandered around the room until they settled on a old iron pot in the corner. Then the door opened and a cruel voice called:

"The great one wants his dinner. You'd better prepare it right this time. He said his carp were too fatty."

"At once!" said Misis' father. I heard a wobble of fear in the old cook's voice.

"Be quick about it. And don't forget the water for the creature."

There was a clatter of pots and pans. I peered through my hole but didn't get a look at the visitor.

Day XXVI

I have much to tell. That night I begged Misis to

leave the door open so that I could get a little air.

"Can I trust you? Father will be angry if you run."

"Don't worry," I said. "I promise I will not leave this night."

She sniffed and gave me one of those sad looks of hers. As night fell, I put a paw to the door. Misis had not bolted the door. So I crept out like a night vole on the hunt for worms, or whatever it is that night voles have for their supper.

Haireena, I am a cat of my word. I'd promised not to make a run for it that night. But I hadn't said anything about escaping in the morning.

I decided to look for the upper deck. The corridor from the galley led to two passages but neither had a ladder.

We warriors of the Kitons hunt by night and never lose our way. Nevertheless, I had been exploring the ship for rather a long time when I made out a light from some unknown cabin. There is something about a light in the darkness, Haireena. Though I knew of the danger, I just couldn't stop myself from padding towards it.

As I approached, I spotted a ladder at the end of the corridor. At last, a way to the upper decks! There was nothing for it but to creep past the cabin with the light. The door was half-open as I sneaked past, so I couldn't resist a peek inside.

It wasn't a cabin but a wide open space. I tasted

burning at the back of my throat and it was all that I could do to stop myself choking.

Inside was a sight that would chill the seeds out of most warrior's marrows. A freakish figure stood pawing over an enormous map. He was half in shadow. A leather bucket and a stone pot sat on a low table. Strange sounds were coming from that bucket. The giant took up the pot in one of his great paws and set it spinning on the table.

"Bring me the flame!" he called.

A female appeared, holding a torch. Just behind her was a guard, armed with a three-pointed spear. The giant took the flaming torch from the female and cast it into the spinning pot.

"Make the magic work this time, or I'll stick you with this!" hissed the little one with the trident.

I gasped – fearing for the poor female – but then I realised that the guard seemed to be talking to the bucket!

"Wait," said the giant. "It begins."

The pot span faster and faster until sparks shot across the room. Strange lights flickered. Shadows danced and pictures appeared.

Then the female began to dance. As she moved, the fire shone through the holes in the pot and I saw pictures appear on the walls.

I'm not the sort of cat who is easily impressed by magic. At school they were always going on about the gateways between this world and the next but I never paid much attention. I was too busy thinking about my lyre or my bone collection. If you ask me, there's nothing duller than listening to the old ones of our tribe when they start going on about the 'visions' that they have seen. If an elder has seen a vision, it's a sure sign that either they want something from you or the plant they call 'catnip' is in season, if you know what I mean.

But this was different Haireena. I swear that I saw pictures dancing across the walls.

First I saw a band of soldiers in white robes, riding upon strange beasts to a stone fortress on top of a cliff. The soldiers went into the mouth of a cave.

Now I must tell the strangest thing of all. As the female danced I got a clear sight of her face in the torchlight. Haireena, it was you.

I was about to call out to you but a paw on my shoulder broke the spell and a voice whispered:

"Make no sound. To be in this room is forbidden. Follow me."

Can it be that you are here on this very ship Haireena? Or did I call you up from my memory, to dance in my vision? I can think of nothing else.

As Misis led me back to the galley, I felt shamed. I'd given my word that I would not try to escape and she had caught me at it. She opened the door of the hold for me to climb back into my hiding place once more. As I stood on the edge, my heart sank.

"Misis, wait. I am sorry..." I began.

"You will be!" said a voice from the shadows. I saw that her father lay in wait for me. He had the lickamen barrel open, and beside it, a hammer and nails. Misis gasped.

"What were you thinking? Going into that cabin is forbidden."

"I didn't know that. I must have just blundered into it by mistake," I answered.

The old cook's eyes flashed.

"So, you 'blundered' out of a locked hold into a hidden chamber, on a secret deck?"

"That's right," I said.

"Well blunderer! If I did not know better, I'd have taken you for a spy. Get back in your barrel."

"I'm not a spy," I answered, my bristles rising.

"Get in," ordered the cook, with a flick of the tail. I had no choice. So I climbed back into the barrel.

"We Kitons are known for our fair-play. We don't do secrets."

"We don't do secrets!" he laughed. "Don't take me for a fool. I've travelled in your land. 'We do not do secrets indeed!' What were you up to in that room Mewid? Sniffing for secrets I'll guess."

Now Haireena, the Mewids are the white-robbed priests of the Land of the Kitons. They buy and sell secrets. From hearing how they speak about us Kitons in Rome, you would think that every ginger-furred cat was a Mewid sorcerer or a spy.

"I cannot sleep safe with you in my galley. Have

you got a little sliver blade packed away somewhere?" hissed the cook.

"I'm not a Mewid! I hate them and all they stand for." I answered.

Misis padded close to me and sniffed the air. Then she shook her head sadly.

"Lies!" hissed the cook. "She can smell them."

He snatched up the hammer and told his daughter to fetch the lid.

"Wait!" I cried." "If you must know, I did want to be a Mewid. To learn music, not magic. But my mother would not allow it. She can't stand them.

"Good," said the cook, nodding. He placed the hammer carefully on the deck. "We have the truth at last. Tell me Kiton, what were you doing in that room?"

"It was an accident!" I cried. "I was trying to sneak overboard."

"Understand this. We are on the open sea – and to jump overboard would mean certain death."

"I know!" I answered. "I did not mean to swim. I am not that much of a fool. I meant to throw myself over in a barrel."

"And float back to Rome? You must have made some deal with Fortuna! That I cannot believe!" he said sadly, picking up the hammer once more.

Misis suddenly sprang to my defence.

"Wait, father!" she cried.

She padded over, pressed her nose to my maw and

began to sniff. Well, I can tell you I did not like her nosing around my mouth like that. Even though I am particular about my teeth and clean them every week, whether they need it or not.

"There is no lie on his breath father," said Misis.

She'd saved me. But the old cook looked puzzled.

"Why risk your life, adrift in a barrel?"

There was only one true answer, so I decided he may as well hear it.

"The one I love was given to a gladiator by the Emperor. Although he's twice my size, and a trained killer, I've vowed to find them and set her free."

On hearing these words, Misis sprang up from her place and flew from the room in tears.

"Forget about floating back," he said. "It is two hundred leagues back to Rome. You'll need to find a ship. We will help, when we make port."

"My thanks," I said. "But there is more that I must say. Maybe it was the magic of that chamber – but I'm sure I saw my love in that room. She was dancing for the giant. Perhaps I dreamed her, or her ghost is following me across the sea. But if she's alive on this ship, I've got to find her."

"Wait here!" said the cook. "I must go after my daughter."

At the doorway, he stopped. "What is the name of this female? The one you would risk everything for?"

"Haireena," I replied.

His laughter shook the room.

AUGUSTPUSS XVIII

August 18th

Poor Jebel

This day is one of the saddest in my life, which sets a sad standard. Today, I must record that poor Jebel is dead. Somehow, the fresh water in his pail was changed for salt water. So he died soon after.

How this has happened, I cannot say. I suspect the Mate, for he has a particular loathing for frogs. I admit that I used to dislike them too, but I grew very fond of ours.

Eddipuss asked the Mate about it but he was ordered back to his post. He says we cannot lose sight of the ship with red sails. My heart is heavy. We will bury Jebel at dawn.

AUGUSTPUSS XIX

August 19th

The sea was flat and the sky was grey, like a pewter plate.

"Poor Jebel!" I said. "His little life has ended. He dreamed of returning to his mistress. But he died so far away from his home," sniffed Eddipuss.

"I'll just put him down here. The tide can take him

to his last resting place."

"Er, Eddipuss. Wait a moment," I protested. But he had already picked up my cushion and reached into the bucket.

"This cushion is from the Land of the Kush – Jebel's home. It is fitting to lay him to rest on it."

"No, I beg you! That cushion is a present for my wife. And if I ever return from this disaster without a present, my already blighted life will be of no worth."

"We can't just throw him over the side," said Eddipuss. "It does not seem fair."
I thought on the matter for a while. I did not have the heart to cast him to the fish.

"I know!" I said, with a lump in my throat. "We'll set him adrift in this pot."

"Yes, the pot!" sniffed Eddipuss. "What did he used to say? This pot will lead you to great riches. He was always going on about his Mistress and her treasure. Perhaps the pot will bring him riches in his next life."

So we placed the body of the frog into the pot, lowered it slowly over the side of the ship and said our last goodbyes.

I looked out at the waves and wondered.

"I suppose that I am also doomed to die without a coin to my name, in a land where I am known by nobody, with no son to survive me."

As if commanded by Neptuna himself, a sea bird let

out a loud and mournful cry. Then Eddipuss let out a louder one.

"The pot!" he hissed.

I looked at Eddipuss, and he looked back at me. We were both thinking the same thing.

"Jump! In Paws name! You must go, for I cannot swim," he cried.

I sprang over the side after the pot. It was half under water, but it had not yet sunk. I am no great swimmer, and I splashed around in vain.

"Grab it! By Maul's Mangy Maw! Get a hold of that pot. It'll lead us to the frog's mistress and her treasure!"

The water was colder than an ice plunge. The waves, which had looked puny from the safety of the deck, were a lot bigger when they broke up your nose.

Curses rang from above. The Mate had heard Eddi shouting and come to do some shouting of his own.

"By Neptune's Pointy Fork! What are you doing here? Didn't I tell you to keep those fine eyes of yours on the ship with the red sails?"

"Help!" cried Eddi. "Spartapuss is drowning!"

"Good!" growled the Mate. "If that ginger squab fell off the deck on a sea this flat, then he deserves to drown."

"Help! What can I do?" cried Eddipuss in a panic.

"Leave him to the sharks, and get back to your post," answered the Mate. "I told you not to take your eyes off that red sail."

"Wait! There's treasure! Help us get the pot!" spluttered Eddi. "You can have a third share of it." The Mate let out a low hiss.

"All right. You can have a half share then!" said Eddi.

On hearing this, the Mate went wilder still. I could even hear his curses from where I floundered in the waves. What had upset him so? I had no clue.

An unexpected swell swept me close to the side of the boat. With an enormous stretch, I just managed to get a claw hold on it.

"For Peus sake, throw me a line!" I cried. I was soaked to the bones and my beautiful coat clung to me like weed on a toad's flipper.

Eddipuss let down a thin rope, which I finally got hold of.

Now reader, I would not say that I am 'fat' – although my wife would disagree. I have however, grown rather wider around the middle than I was in the lean days of my youth, when I fought in the arena. Indeed, a neighbour recently bought a trident as a souvenir and I offered to show him a few moves with it. I thrust the long spear out in the way of the gladiator, when my son called:

"Dropped your sausage again father? I'd leave the cooking to mother if I were you?"

So you can understand that I feared to trust my life to such a thin rope. I have never been a confident climber.

"Are you sure it will hold me?" I shouted over the roar of the spray.

"Not you! Send up the pot!" came the reply.

At last, Eddi found a stronger rope and with some difficulty, my shipmate heaved me up onto the deck.

"Don't flap like a flounder," cried the Mate. "Get back to your station! And keep your eyes on that red sail."

On saying this, the Mate sprang off towards the tiller in a huff. But he tripped over the pot. For a sailor he is clumsy. He pawed at it, running his claws around the rim. Luckily it was not broken.

"What by the Cyclaw's Good Eye is this?" said the Mate. "I told you not to move things around!" he hissed.

"Sorry!" said Eddipuss. "That's our pot."

"I know what it is," said the Mate.

"The frog said it could lead us to great riches," said Eddi. The Mate did not seem surprised to hear of a talking frog.

"Where did you come by this? This can't belong to you."

"It certainly does!" I said. "I paid good gold for it, in the market in Ostia."

"This is from the Kingdom of the Kushionites," said the Mate, running his paw carefully over the pot. "I can't believe you got it in a market."

"The frog said it would lead us to treasure. Light a

fire! Then you'll see if I'm speaking the truth. "

"Light a fire? On a ship?" hissed the mate. "Who ever heard of such a thing?"

Now when you hear someone say something that is not true, it is sometimes very hard to hold your tongue. Especially if he has a habit of calling you a 'ginger squab' six or seven times a day.

"I have heard of such a thing," I answered. "The writer Pusspero tells of the fire-ships that sailed to Tray. I am surprised you didn't know this, seeing as you are an experienced sailor."

"NO ONE SAILS A FIRE SHIP!" hissed the Mate, back to his old raging ways. I soon learned that a 'fire ship' is a captured ship which is set alight and then set adrift in the direction of the enemy fleet. I cannot write down exactly what was said, in case this diary falls into the paws of younger readers. Shall we say that having heard the Mate say his piece, I was satisfied that no sailor would turn their own ship into a 'fire ship' on purpose.

"You useless ginger squab!" he hissed when he was finished.

"Wait!" cried Eddipuss. I know where we can get a fire going!"

At that moment there was a terrible crack – so loud that it would shake Mewpiter, the Lord of Thunder from his tree on Mount Olympuss. Leaving the matter of the fire aside, we all rushed from the galley and sprang to the deck.

A sudden storm had blown up and the 'Mare' was raging. Loose ropes, caught by the wind, hissed across the deck. I saw the ship's tiller swing this way and that, as if gripped by invisible paws.

Now *The Lepida* was adrift. I had a terrible thought. Had Fortune decided that we would sink now? What if my gold was aboard.

As Eddipuss climbed up the mast to wrestle with the sails, I decided to check the Captain's cabin.

"Captain?" I called. "All paws on deck!"

There had been no sight of the Captain throughout the whole voyage, but I wanted to check the cabin for my gold and this was my chance.

"Save your breath," said a voice at my side. It was the Mate. "He cannot hear you."

Back on deck the wind was howling. High above me, a dot clung to a swinging mast. It was Eddipuss. With one claw on the rigging, he wrestled with the tangle.

"Almost done!" he called. Then he lost his hold and fell. I feared that he would drop to the deck like a stone. But somehow, he stuck out a paw and got hold of the sail. There he swung, spinning in the wind, like a spider on a thread.

"Are you done yet?" called the Mate, who seemed not to have noticed the fall. "Get a move on, or we'll loose the sail."

"Help!" cried Eddipuss. "I think my leg is broken."

I looked at the Mate. I am a cat of some considerable years. Even in my youth I was no great climber. As the ship lurched from side to side, I shivered at the thought of the height. The climb might be the death of me.

"Get up there and help him," said the Mate.

"My paws are weak. You are the experienced sailor. I fear that I am no great climber..." I began.

"Go. He needs your help," he replied. "Take this," he said, placing a long coil of rope in my paw.

My heart was beating like a war drum as I began the climb. I inched my way upwards, taking care not to look down, as the deck rocked below me. Each movement made me prickle with fear.

As I reached the beam where Eddipuss clung on, an iron hook flew off and crashed to the deck below. It landed inches from the Mate but he didn't flinch.

Eddi hung on bravely. His right leg dangled limp. At last I got the rope around him.

"Have you got him yet?" called the Mate.

"For Peus Sake! I'm going as fast as I can!" I answered.

"Throw the rope over the crossbeam. Tie it on, then lower him gently," came his reply.

Although the advice was of great value, I was astonished at this. He, the experienced sailor, had refused the climb, but now he shouted out his advice. Was our Mate mad, or was this some kind of test? His moods swung from kindness to spite, as the deck swayed below me.

AUGUSTPUSS XX

August 20th

Tonight the Mate joined us in the galley. The storm has blown itself out. Eddipuss was nursing his damaged leg, but he was otherwise in good cheer.

"Thank you, for saving me!" he said, happily. "Although I prayed to Slipus, the God of Long Drops, I couldn't have held on much longer. I was about to let slip moorings."

"Sorry I took so long. But I am too old for climbing and and I have a terror of high places."

Whilst saying this I looked at the Mate. For I remembered what he'd said about the Captain not being able to hear me. Something terrible must have happened. An argument that ended with the Captain at the bottom of the sea.

The Mate's head sank to the deck and he crouched low to the ground.

"You two may as well know it," he said.

For a moment I thought that he was about to confess to the terrible crime. But instead he turned to Eddipuss: "We're lost," he moaned.

Eddipuss has an amazing talent for saying precisely the wrong thing, at exactly the wrong time. And before I could stop him, he set off again down this road.

"Why not ask the Captain where we are?" said Eddi. "He's bound to have maps and things."

I shuddered. The Mate was in a dark mood.

"Impossible!" he hissed.

"Why?" asked Eddipuss.

"The Captain was lost, long ago. We'll never catch them now."

"Catch who?" asked Eddipuss.

"That ship with red sails," I said.

The Mate nodded. I had guessed right, although I still had no clue why we were chasing them.

"So – we've lost the red-sailed ship. But can't you use the stars to guide our way?"

"I can't," moaned the Mate. The voice that had once boomed out orders now stuck in his throat. Eddipuss of course, had not noticed his distress.

"Why not? Don't all sailors know how to steer by the stars?"

The Mate let out a frustrated sigh.

"Why not have a go?" asked Eddipuss.

"Because I'm blind" hissed the Mate.

And with that he turned tail and padded sadly towards the door.

The fog had lifted and now I began to understand. That is why the Mate did not want to climb the mast and rescue Eddipuss. With the rigging in a tangle he could no longer climb about by memory.

"Blind! How can you be blind?" asked Eddipuss.

"It was the Captain's gift for my years of service," said the Mate in a half-hiss.

Eddi and I came close and looked. There was not the slightest sign of his blindness, apart from a little cloudiness in his cold green eyes.

"You look alright to me. Why don't you get a healer to have a look?" asked Eddi.

"I did," said the Mate. "He told me it's poison from a sea spine."

Eddipuss winced.

"There's no cure," he added, before Eddi could get another silly question out.

"Say no more about it," he said finally.

"There is one thing I do not understand. If you are blind, how do you manage to get about the ship so fast?" asked Eddi.

"I carry a map in my mind. I follow my nose and I keep out of the way of half-witted squabs like you," shouted the Mate. His temper at least seemed to be back to normal.

"Well," I said, "Since we cannot sail by the stars, we must trust to the goddess Fortune. She is blind too, they say."

THE SECRET DIARY OF S.O.S

Day XXVII

As I lay hidden in my cupboard on board the ship I was woken up by a loud scratching on the door.

"It's probably just Misis," I thought. Rolling over, I decided to ignore it.

"Get up ginger one!" boomed a voice.

"All right! Keep your fur on!" I called.

The sort of thing that happens every morning isn't going to make me leap off my cushion with excitement. I have been on this ship for more days than I can count, and the most exciting thing has been a rat in the biscuit barrel – and that turned out to be a woodmouse.

"Get up Kiton!" called the voice again.

"No thanks," I answered.

"We are home at last," called Misis. "Come and see!"

"No Misis. It is too dangerous," boomed the cook. "He must stay below. He can slip ashore tonight."

I didn't get it. Why couldn't I have a look on deck? We'd made port, so they could hardly throw me overboard! I'd soon talked Misis into letting me have a peak at her homeland. When her father had gone we sneaked up to see what was going on.

"This shore is a bit of a bore," I said, as we took in the view. I'd heard lots of tales about the land of Fleagypt so I was expecting amazing sights. The

Purramids, the roar of the mighty Nile river.

But all I got was a view of the back of the docks. The moaning wind carried small grains of brown sand that caught in my throat and got stuck in my pads.

"Curse this desert wind!" I said, brushing it out of my coat. "I expect you are used to it, being a cat of the desert."

"That is not the desert wind. It's a breeze from the beach," said Misis.

"Are you sure?" I asked. "It's very gritty."

"I'm sure. Most of my people live in the towns anyway," she said.

"Really?" I replied. She must have caught the disappointment in my voice.

"Excuse me! I must go and tend to my thousand camels," she hissed, padding off in a sulk.

I was surprised, for I didn't know there were any camels on the ship. Then I realised that was her idea of a joke. There is no understanding females sometimes so I begged her to come back. She returned and took her place next to me. From the spot where we were hiding, we had a good view of the deck. All of the passengers pawed at their luggage while great crates of cargo were taken ashore.

I noticed that our crew were singing a song called 'Paws away' but sitting on theirs, and not doing a stroke of work. Some local cats in colourful robes had come aboard. They hauled at the ropes whilst the sea cats looked on. Money passed from paw to paw.

Misis looked miserble as usual.

"It is interesting what you notice when you are a traveller in a strange land," I said, hoping I could cheer her up. "I've noticed that the locals are wearing unusually bright collars. Some are blue and some are red. It is a shame I don't have my lyre. I could write a song about this: 'The Multi-Coloured Collars of the Cats of Fleagypt's Land' or something."

"They are slaves," said Misis sadly. "Those collars tell their masters who they belong to."

"Slaves?" I said in surprise. But they are so well dressed. I'd not heard they had slaves in this land."

"Who do you think builds the great tombs for the Furroahs?" she asked.

"Now that's a I job I wouldn't mind doing," I replied. "If I had to be a slave, of course. It beats cleaning out the vomitorium. They might also get to do some stone carving. I've done a bit of that myself."

"Thousands die in the construction," said Misis. "Their names are not carved on the Furroh's tombs. They sleep nameless, under the sands."

"Sorry," I said. "My own father was a slave once. I didn't mean any offence."

I'll say one thing for Misis, she certainly knows how to make you think. It's a shame she's so gloomy all the time. If the Emperor gave a prize at the Games for moping, she would beat off all comers!

I decided to change the subject once more.

"Why don't the sailors help them unload?" I

asked.

"They are betting on which team will unload the most: the Reds or the Blues." said Misis.

I was about to ask her which side she fancied when an terrible boom shook the ship.

A heavy crate had fallen to the deck. I heard cries. One of the Reds was trapped. A sailor sprang up to help but to my surprise, he was warned off with a hiss.

"What are they doing? Why won't they help?"

"Everyone has placed their bets," said Misis, spitting the word out like a bad bit of rat. "The gang-master has a lot of money on the Blues."

Anger awoke within me. I couldn't stand to see another cat suffer. The next thing I knew, I was spring-ing across the deck. The crew were surprised – they even stopped cursing! I leapt over to the fallen crate, and tried to free the poor fellow.

The crowd of sailors began to hiss and jeer and the air was filled with shouts in strange tongues. I got a grip on the edge of the crate and heaved with the strength of a warrior.

But I couldn't shift it. As I hauled, I felt everyone's eyes upon me. Misis was watching from her hiding place.

"Leave it Ginger! Get your paws off," hissed a tabby.

"Don't listen to him. Put your back into it!" laughed another who was backing the other side.

Not one of them would lift a paw to help. The fellow's

cries grew weaker.

Then the deck went as quiet as the tomb – and the crate grew suddenly lighter. It began to rise into the air, as if it was charmed. It was all that I could do to hang onto my end of it, and keep it off the poor slave's tail. At last the crate was set gently back on the deck, and the slave was free.

When he was clear, I heard a voice cry:

"Why are you sailors standing around? Get busy and help them. We have a timetable to keep."

From around the other side of the crate stepped a giant of a cat. The same one I'd had seen in the Emperor's Golden House, and again in the cabin where you danced for him, Haireena. Why hadn't I recognised him? I do not know.

I should have flown at him right then for stealing you away. He was bigger than I remembered, but it wasn't his size that stayed my paw. Before I could challenge him, he thanked me:

"Well done! At least there are two of us aboard who know not to laugh when a fellow needs help."

The brute's voice was clear and kind, if a little bit high in pitch. I wanted to answer him, but the words kind of stuck in my throat and I could only nod.

"Can you believe that our crew dare to call these locals 'savages?'" he added.

Then the crowd parted, and he marched towards the gang-master, clutching a list in his enormous paw. The time to act had come and gone but I had stood by and done nothing. I still burn with the shame of it.

I couldn't stay on board after what had happened. I didn't have the heart to say goodbye, so I slipped ashore without another word to Misis. Somehow it seemed worse that she was there to see what a coward I am.

I decided to crawl under a stone, or throw myself into the river for the hungry crocodiles. But there weren't any stones, just sandy streets. I couldn't even find the great river, so instead I followed the crowds from the docks to the town.

The locals chattered fast and I understood no word of what they were saying. It was like listening to a swarm of bees. The buzzing got louder as the streets narrowed. I padded on through the tangle of roads until at last the maze opened into a courtyard where fat faced merchants lay around on cushions. I felt a paw at my collar and a thin grey sniffed at me and called me into one of the shops that ringed the square.

The air was thick with blue smoke, and all the time, the locals were jabbering at me to buy who knows what.

When they found I had no money, they cursed me and left. Then an amber-eyed fellow returned to trade with me. He had no Catin but soon, by means of signs, I'd sold my collar for a few coins.

With coins in paw, I was treated like a king! Plate after plate and bowl after bowl were brought before me. I had no stomach for the food and the brew had a foul second taste to it. I tried to get them to take it back but they laughed and brought me more. After the third bowl, I was used to the aftertaste.

How many hours passed, I cannot say. At last, the owner approached and pressed his nose close to mine, so that I could feel his foul breath on my whiskers. The room began to spin. I pulled out my last coin but he threw it back in my face. I tried to spring at him but I wobbled and fell to the ground. Then a cat with a long knife emerged from the kitchen and gave me a scratch on my face. I didn't feel any pain.

"Awake!" said a familiar voice. As I came to my senses, I could smell the night air. Blinking like a new-born kitten, I squeezed my sticky eyes open.

"Misis?" I groaned. "What are you doing here?"

"Pawrus be praised!" she said. "You're alive. How do you feel?"

Well, I did not tell her, but I had never felt so low.

"Never felt better," I said. "Don't worry. You can go now."

"I can't do that," she smiled. "Till you give me an honest answer."

Fortune had cursed me by hooking me up with the one female in the Feline Empire who has an uncanny knack of knowing when I'm not telling the truth.

"So be it," I continued. "If you must know Misis, I'm not all right. For I don't have the courage to fight for what is mine."

"I don't understand. Why did you run away?"

"Remember the giant who helped me free the slave from under that crate?" I mumbled. She nodded.

"I recognised him..." I stuttered over my words, and began to cough. She produced a bag and pressed it to my lips. The water was fresh, if a little warm.

"His name is Spitulus," said Misis. "They call him 'The Educated Gladiator'. Father ordered me to say nothing of it. But the whole ship is talking about him and his mission."

"I see," I added, trying not to sound concerned. "Why do they call him that?" I asked.

"It is said that he can speak Squeak as well as Catin. And another language – Furracian – I think."
I hated Spitulus even more now.

"An 'Educated Gladiator'. Just want we need! That'll be useful in the Arena. When he sends his opponents into to the next world he can bid them farewell in four different tongues."

"Well – it could be worse," said Misis softly.

"How could it be worse?" I hissed. "My sworn enemy is taller than me, stronger than me and richer than me. Now I learn that he is also educated."

"At least he didn't recognise you. Father says his eyes are failing – that's why he gave up the arena."

Although I did not tell her, I was angry because talking to the brute made it harder for me to hate him. By the way he helped me to free that poor slave, I might be able to add 'kindness' to the long list of his good points.

Misis told me to get up and I began to pad about a bit. She watched in silence as I stretched my claws and walked in a circle. At last she spoke in a soft voice:

"This Haireena – are you sure she's worth it?"

"She's everything!" I replied, moving faster now. "Gladiator or not, I must confront Spitulus and find out what he's done to Haireena. If he has harmed a single fur of her coat, I'll give him an education. Gladiator or not!"

A crowd had gathered. I began to shake with rage.

"Do you really want to find her?" said Misis. The sadness about her was back again.

"Absolutely!" I said. "Can't you tell I mean it?" She nodded, backing away.

"Well, there is no time to waste. Spitulus and his party left at dawn. Your Haireena is with them."

My heart was in my mouth. I looked at her in wonder.

"Is this some vision you've seen?" I gasped.

"The whole ship saw them leave," she said. "They are on an expedition for the Emperor. Ask on the road for a party of twenty camels.

Then she threw me a bag full of coins.

"My thanks forever. Why are you doing this?" "No questions," she replied. "I know you'll pay me back."

I grabbed the water skin and sprang down the road.

"Wait!" she called. "You'll need more water than that. At least five skins. One for each day on the road."

"Of course!" I answered. "I know that."

She looked at me, and from her eyes I could tell that she wanted me to invite her to come along.

"You can't follow them without a camel."

"I know that," I said. "Where can I find one?"

She took me through the city to the south road. On the way we bought some more water skins. Misis insisted that they were filled in the shop and checked that they did not leak.

On we went, through the outskirts of town until at last we came to a series of wooden posts, hammered into the sand. Each post had a sign with a mark – the name of the camel trader

"Father says that Pawrus is honest. His post is the at the far end," she said.

She offered to wait until later that afternoon, for the camel market would not open in the heat of the sun. She gave me a lot of advice about camels, so much that I could not believe a young female should be so knowledgeable about them. In my land it is the dream of every young female to have a chariot pony of her own, to boss around. Perhaps it is the same with camels for the females of this land?

"Never buy a beast that has red eyes, for he may be suffering from fever," she said. "And always be sure to have a good look at the teeth."

"Why?" I asked. "They don't need sharp teeth. They're not savage creatures are they?"

"If your camel's teeth are bad, he cannot eat. If he cannot eat, he will die," she sighed.

Though she begged to stay and help me strike a good bargain, I begged her to leave. In truth I could stand no more of her advice. As she turned back to the port, she called:

"Make sure that the beast sits at your command and follows orders."

I didn't have long to wait, for soon after I lost sight of her in the red dust, an old trader appeared. He tied up three camels to the middle post. Then he greeted me in four different languages.

"Can I help you, my friend?" he asked.

I'm no fool. I wasn't about to buy the first camel I saw. Besides, I still had one thousand and one facts on camels from Misis buzzing in my brain.

"I'm waiting for Pawrus," I said. "Any idea how long he'll be?"

When he heard me speak, he sprang over and greeted me like a long lost friend.

"I am Pawrus, my Roman friend," he cried. "And if it is relics of the dead that you have come for, you are in luck. The sands to the south are thick with treasures."

"No treasures thanks, I want a camel," I said.

"Why didn't you say?" he beamed. "Step this way."

I've never bought a camel before but I think I've done quite well. During the sale, a crowd gathered to offer me advice.

At first he tried to sell me a dark-haired brute that towered above me. The crowd were all pointing at it and smiling and saying it was the best. But when Pawrus opened its mouth to show me its teeth, the camel spat at me. The crowd laughed.

"It is normal," said the trader. But I wasn't going to be fooled. It had an enormous hump – some kind of horrible hump disease I expect. So I waved it away and he showed me some more beasts. I liked the look of a small one.

"That one is a baby, no good for desert trips," said a voice from the crowd.

"Let him choose!" hissed the trader, "He needs no help from you."

I chose the small one and they tied my water skins on tight. I also bought warm clothes, wood, a couple of stakes and some dried food for the journey.

"Which way is the river?" I asked. "I'm hoping to find the Romans who set off yesterday"

The trader pointed at a wide track leading away from the city. At least there was no chance of getting lost. He whistled and the camel sat down. Then he helped me onto its back.

"Pawrus keep you safe from Nomats!" he said.

"Nomats?" I asked. The crowd fell silent as the Furroah's stone tomb.

I remember the fear in Misis' eyes when she'd warned me about the Nomats. She'd begged me to travel as near to the river as possible. For along the great Nile were many villages and even some traders who spoke my own language. I asked about the route to the river.

"It is a two hour ride," said the trader. "Be sure you find it before darkness falls."

I pulled on the rope and my camel began to walk.

Day XXIX

As I write, the sun falls and the sand spreads out like red waves. My camel is having a rest. I haven't found you Haireena, but I am on your trail. I have decided not to put up a tent. The cool breeze makes a change from the burning of the day's sun. How cold can it get in the desert?

Day XXX

Last night I nearly froze my claws off. I got no sleep at all. There is no time to write much today Haireena. My new camel is a moody beast. I have decided to call her Misis – after another gloomy female that I met on my travels.

Day XXXI

I have still not found the river road. I can't understand it. I should have found it yesterday. My camel has been walking slowly for hours. I offered to share my food with her today but she gave me a funny look.

Her hump has gone all floppy. Misis warned me about floppy humps. If only I could remember.

Day XXXII

That ungrateful beast trod on my water skins and burst them with her hoof! Today both she and I must walk without water. I must find the river.

Day XXXIII

Set Misis loose. Faster without her. I see your face in the sands. I see his too.

Goodbye Haireena.

AUGUSTPUSS XXI

August 21st

Secrets and Flies

The next morning, the wind dropped and we got busy with repairs to the ship. The Mate was in a foul mood, for the storm had knocked everything from its usual place. It's amazing that he can hold every detail about the ship in his memory. I have trouble remembering where I put the cream in my own kitchen!

When our tasks were done, the Mate told us to meet him in the galley. Eddipuss got a fire going, and I fetched the black pot. Eddi had soon stoked up a good fire and we placed the pot in front of it.

"Wait!" said Eddipuss in a whisper.

Nothing happened.

"Wait!" said Eddipuss once more.

"We are waiting," I sighed. "It's no use."

"The frog told us to spin it," said Eddi.

I gave it a good spin. Still nothing happened

"Set the thing on its base," said the Mate.

Eddipuss did just as he was told.

"Does the firelight shine through it?" asked the Mate.

"Yes," I replied.

"Wait!" cried Eddi. Are we still spinning it so it will

lead us to Jebel's Mistress's treasure?"

"You'd better pray that it'll lead us to land," said the Mate.

"Please can we get on with this?" I sighed. For it was hot in the galley from the blaze of the cooking fire and the air was thick. With a crew of only three, the decks do not get swabbed as often as one might like.

"Wait!" said Eddi. "What about poor Jebel? We cannot spin the pot with him still inside. It is unlucky!"

"It might be more unlucky to take him out!" I said. The very thought was so unpleasant that I put my paws in front of my eyes.

"I do not fear the dead," said the Mate. And he thrust his paw into the pot, picked up the little bundle containing our friend and set it down on the cushion.

"Let it spin!" cried the Mate, and he sent the pot spinning with a swipe of the paw.

As the black pot turned, the firelight began to shine through the holes on its rim. Shadows danced on the galley walls.

Then the most incredible thing happened. Those you who believe in pawtents, or are scared of the magic of the ancients, might wish to skip this next part of my diary.

For in that hot room, the three of us heard a sound that chilled us to our bones. It was a muffled croaking sound, at first very faint but soon it became louder and louder. It was coming from the cushion. I looked down and saw the little bundle hopping up and down.

"Aaaagh!" cried Eddipuss. "What sorcery is this?"

"Get it off, get it off!" I cried. "That cushion is a present for my wife!"

"I'll gladly get off, when you free me from this bundle!" croaked a familiar voice.

"Jebel?" cried Eddipuss. "Can it be you?"

"How many talking frogs do you know?" I asked.

"By the Titan's teeth!" cried the Mate. "The frog talks!"

"Get me out of here for I am hotter than Hades' housekeeper wrapped up in this parcel!" said Jebel.
Soon we had him free and the first thing he called for was water.

"Be sure to give him fresh water this time!" said Eddi.

The Mate looked shame-faced. "I am sorry!" he said.

"I could no longer stand the taste of the cursed 'frog water' stew you keep feeding us," said the Mate. "I thought a little salt might improve the taste of it."

"What do you mean?" asked Jebel.

"Ssssh!" I said to Eddipuss. "Say nothing about it yet as it may be a shock."

"That's right. Frogs are sensitive creatures. We don't want to kill him again," said Eddi.

"What?" croaked Jebel.

THE SECRET DIARY OF S.O.S.

Day I

Well, I call it 'Day I' as I've lost count of the days. So much has happened since I was taken that night.

I can't remember much about my last hours of freedom. I remember setting my camel loose when she could carry me no longer. Then I walked till my pads began to burn.

At my last gasp, I dragged myself up the face of a dune, my paw hit upon something hard amongst the sand. It was a pile of old bones. As I lay down to die, I wondered if it would be a puzzle for the explorers of future. Two sets of bones all mixed up together. Would they be looking for a two-headed desert cat?

I woke to the taste of water on my lips, and they had to hold me back to stop me from drinking too fast in case my insides burst. I passed out again, and when they woke me, they led me to a large tent.

It was night time, and a hunter's moon was high in the sky, although the stars were strange. The night air was full of drums and a high ringing sound. They led me past a rock. Twenty dancers were beating it with sticks until it rang like a caldron being struck with a hammer. As the drummers beat out time, the warriors danced inside a circle in the sand. There was little joy in their dance, only menace.

As they led me past, I could see their steps form

patterns in the sand.

At last we reached the tent of the leader of the Nomats – for as you have guessed, they had found me wandering in the desert.

I don't know for sure that he was their leader, but I should guess it, because his tent was filled with fine hangings and great jars made of black stone.

My guard fixed me with a stare and prodded me with a stick. Then the leader said some words to me in his own tongue. I thought I heard him say: "Friends?" in Catin, but I'm not certain.

I remembered my father's advice about speaking to strangers in a different tongue.

He said that if you do not know what a foreigner is saying, you must simply smile, nod and answer 'yes' to every question that you are asked. That way, you cannot offend anyone.

I followed that advice and woke up tied to a stake, in the burning heat. With the effort of Hercatules I managed to turn my head. Through sand-blind eyes, I saw that another cat was tied up next to me. He was half dead with thirst. With a great effort, I called out to him.

When he turned towards me to answer my cries I saw the face of Spitulus, my sworn enemy. He must also have been captured by the Nomats. I don't think he recognised me, but he seemed glad of the company.

"The cruelty of these rats," he gasped. "Tying us up

so close to the Nile, so that we die of thirst with the scent of water in our noses."

"I raised my head as far as the ropes would allow, and then wished that I hadn't.

"I don't think death from thirst is what they've got in mind for us," I hissed.

An enormous crocodile was lumbering towards us from the river. It's great belly was fat from long years of hunting. It moved slowly, as if it knew it didn't need to hurry.

Spitulus began to bellow and shout. He rattled at the chain that held him to his stake. The crocodile stopped and turned its great head towards us.

"What are you doing?" I asked.

"Attracting its attention," he replied.

"What's your plan?" I hissed, wondering how he was going to defeat such a beast.

I looked up again. The creature set off again, dragging itself towards us. Spitulus shook his head sadly.

"My translator is over there," he said. "I must draw the animal away from her."

"Hold your tongue!" I said. "You might want to give up your life for another but I..."

Then I had a terrible thought.

"What's the name of this translator?" I asked.

"Haireena," he replied.

In a rage, I shook my chains until my pads were raw.

"Haireena!" I called. "Don't worry, we will draw

the beast away from you."

Then I bellowed as if my life depended on it – which it did.

The crocodile roared back his answer. I wanted to get a look at what was happening, if only to stare death in the face. With a great effort, I hauled myself up on the chain, craning my neck towards the beast.

Then I laughed for joy.

"What's happening?" cried Spitulus

Now it was close, I saw that the crocodile had an iron collar around its neck. It was held fast on a chain. It pulled and strained but it had reached the end of its leash. There was still a gap of some ten tails' length between the monster and Haireena.

"Why keep a crocodile on a lead?" I laughed. "I didn't know they made good pets!"

Spitulus let out a shriek of excitement.

"I have the answer!" he cried. "They keep it to scare wild crocodiles away from the camp. Caesar wrote that the villagers of the Nile sometimes use this trick. I never thought I would live to see it."

"The Nomats want us alive," I said. "Unless they've got some worse terror in store."

"Under their law we are a gift from the desert," said Spitulus. "They can do what they like with us."

Spitulus was right. For the next ten days they marched us south. We travelled at dusk and walked long into the night. We were treated well and given water and food each day, including fish from the river.

Our route never strayed far from the great Nile.

"This fish isn't bad," I said, picking up a black stone bowl that the guard had left. "Slaves get it easy in this land. No taste of the whip and the cooks know how to roast. Big portions too."

Spitulus laughed.

"They need us strong," he said, tucking into a slab of fish. "What for, I wonder?"

Whenever we reached a new camping place, we dropped exhausted on the sand, letting the drums beat us to sleep.

All this time I longed for a sight of Haireena.

"Their law says that the females must be kept separate from the males," said Spitulus. "Even slaves like us must live by their ways."

On the tenth day we were woken up by a noise in the camp. I ignored it and went back to sleep. When I woke again in the late afternoon, I found that we had company.

The new arrivals were black furred with heavy features. These two had not a word of Catin, and so I didn't know what they were saying.

"What's their story?" I asked, as we tucked into that evening's roasted fish.

"I could find out very little I'm afraid," said Spitulus, spearing a fish with one of his great claws.

"I tried every tongue that I know. All I could learn was that they were travelling to the city of Treebes."

"Treebes?" I said. "Why have I heard of it?"

"The ancients write of it, especially the Squeak poets."

"No, that wasn't it," I said.

A hunk of fish went flying from his bowl and landed on my tail.

"You might talk like a scholar, but you still eat like a gladiator," I laughed.

"Yes," he nodded. "As if every meal could be my last."

We slept through the next day as usual but when the time came to strike camp, no one came for us. Finally, our Nomat guard arrived and led us to the edge of the encampment. The two new arrivals followed close behind as the drums thumped out a march.

I saw that a circle had been marked in the sand. Around it, sat Nomats of all ages, from the youngest kitten to the oldest grey whisker. Each family had set out its tents so that they formed a circle around the ring. In front sat the slaves. I looked for Haireena, but there was no sign of her.

As the drumming started, the slaves sprang into the middle of the circle and the dance began.

"Paws' jaws!" I hissed. "I don't like this. What are they doing?"

"I don't know," said Spitulus. "My eyes aren't that good."

"Looks more like an army drill than a dance."

Before he could answer we were let off the leash.

"This is our chance," I hissed. "Let's run for it."

"Run where?" said Spitulus. "We are in the middle of nowhere. Without water, the desert would soon claim us."

"Suit yourself. I'm going. We won't last long here by the look of this. When the drums stop, the knives will come out. Just watch!"

"Wait!" called Spitulus. "It's not as you say."

Two warriors had been pushed into the centre and now they began to fight.

I know a bit about fighting. I came third in my year at fights, and I only lost out to Mawlus because he got his sister Crushula to sit on me. But I've never seen fighting like this before. The warriors moved with grace. It was a flowing dance, not a hacking, scratching scuffle as it is back home in the Land of the Kitons. At the end, the black and white rolled his opponent over twice and pinned him down in the dust.

The rest of us slaves watching had to practice the roll, which was broken down into slow movements. An old one with a grey ruff moved about the ring, watching to see that we had got it right. All through this, the drums beat out the time.

The drills went on until dawn, and then we were led back to our tents for water and the usual great big helpings of fish and barley biscuits.

"Our training is over for tonight," said Spitulus.

"I don't understand," I whispered. "Training for what? The army?"

"By the look of their art, they can fight their own

battles," said Spitulus. "Did you see the carvings? The soldier king with the leopard at his feet?"

"What then?" I asked as I threw down another great mouthful of roast fish.

"We'll find out soon," said Spitulus.

Now we fell into a different rhythm. We'd travel on one day and train through the next night. All the time we'd follow the line of the river. Each night we learned a new move.

One night the two newcomers to our family were picked out for special training. They began a strange dance. It was all that I could do to stop myself from laughing when a whirlwind came from nowhere and swept through the circle, leaving us all buried up to our ears in sand.

As they led us back to our sleeping place we caught site of the females dancing. Haireena was amongst them, whirling in the middle rank. I was about to spring into the circle and free her, but Spitulus held me back.

"She is alive," said Spitulus. "Just thank whatever god you know for that."

After twenty days, we reached Treebes.

"I thought you said it was a great city," I said, looking at a patch of scrub and a few dusty houses.

"It was great once," said Spitulus. "The Squeak poets write that it had three hundred gates."

"Three hundred flies more like," I said, swatting a monster that had settled on my back before it could draw blood.

"Where are they taking us?" I asked, but there was no time for Spitulus to answer. Our Nomat guards had appeared. By the way their tails flicked, they were on edge.

"They are from the desert, they get nervous in the town," said Spitulus. He was right – every Nomat seemed wound up tight. After the guard had checked our chains, he moved off and I was free to speak.

"There's a crowd over there," I said, peering through the dust. "It's a market! They're going to sell us."

"I think not," said Spitulus, sniffing the dusty air. His great tail began to flick.

"What's wrong?" I asked. "Like you said, it can't be that bad, with the amount of fish and barley biscuits they're feeding us!"

"What do you see over there?"

"Just lots of slaves, hanging about," I answered. "Some of them are wearing palm leaves on their collars."

"They are gladiators," said Spitulus.

"Poor devils," I gasped.

"So are we!" he added.

AUGUSTPUSS XXIV

August 24th

Back from Beyond

Well diary, now I think I've seen it all. Though I rub my eyes with my paws, the living proof hops in front of me, catching mosquitos with his sticky tongue.

After we had got over the shock of getting him back, we had many questions to ask.

"Jebel?" said Eddi checking the water for salt before pouring it in the bucket. "Can I ask something."

"Find me something to eat and you can ask anything! These mosquitos are bitter," said the frog.

Eddi threw a scrap of fish into the bucket and the frog swallowed it whole.

"Did it hurt when you, died?" he asked.

"No," the frog replied. "Not at all."

"What happens then?"

"Nothing happens. You're dead."

Eddipuss gave a disappointed hiss and scratched at his ear. Lowering his voice to a whisper, he spoke:

"I've been told there's a golden road, and it leads to a golden gate. And there stands a golden bull waving at you with his golden hoof..."

"Who told you that?" asked the Mate.

"These fellows I met called 'The Golden Ones'"

said Eddi. "They were very friendly."

"Pay no heed. It sounds like a cult to me," I began. "In my land, it is said there is a place called Summerlands – where the dead go."

"Are all the streets gleaming with gold there?" asked Eddipuss.

"Not as far as I know," I answered.

"Do they have golden rats and mice?" asked Eddi.

"No," I said. "I don't think so."

"What's so special about this 'Summerlands' then? There must be something worth sacrificing for?"

I felt a little ashamed to say, but at last I spoke:

"They say the weather there is always nice."

Eddi stared at me in amazement. The Mate let out a loud laugh. It was the first time I'd heard him laugh.

"That makes no sense," said Eddipuss.

"If you'd lived in The Land of the Kitons, you'd know what I mean," I muttered.

"Well, I can't remember about the weather and I didn't see any gold," said the frog. "I don't think I went anywhere or did anything."

"Surely there must be something?" said Eddipuss.

Jebel did not answer, he went suddenly motionless. Then his red tongue uncoiled and lashed into a fly that had settled on the spillings of a fishbowl. He drew it instantly back into its mouth and there was a crunch as he bit into its body.

"I just stopped," said the frog, with his mouth full.

THE SECRET DIARY OF S.O.S.

Day X

Today I became a gladiator, like my father – if his fireside tales are true. Looking at him now, you'd think he couldn't even finish a pie in the arena!

He told me once of his entrance into the great amphitheatre in Rome. The roar of the crowd and their cruel taste for 'sport'. Well at least he had an actual arena to fight in. We'd been taken to the edge of town where a fighting circle had been roped out for us. It was bare apart from a couple of rain-starved bushes where the 'crowd' were sitting.

Father once told me that gladiators had to 'win the crowd', but you wouldn't want to win this crowd at a dice game. They were no more than twenty in number: rag tags, criminals and mangy loafers. And all of them strangers to the bath house by the smell.

We fighters were brought to the edges of the circle in chains. On the way, I passed an old soldier. By the look of his coat he'd done his full thirty years in the legions.

"Where is everybody?" I asked.

"At the snake show," he laughed. "It's on the other side of town."

"Any advice?" I asked, turning to Spitulus. But the giant looked more nervous than me.

"Make yourself look small. And pray that you are

not chosen today," he said.

"And if I am chosen?" I asked.

"Stay alive," he replied. "Keep away from any fighter wearing a palm leaf."

"Why are they so special?" I asked.

"The palm leaf means they are winners," he answered. "At the games, the winners are killers."

Just then our owner came and dabbed at us with a brush. Spitulus closed his eyes as the brush went over him, but I got an eyeful of red. The paint smelled foul.

"Red. My lucky colour," sighed Spitulus. "One more thing. This is a team game, so remember not to kill anyone in red!"

Although the sun beat down as hard as ever, I felt cold and my insides began to churn.

"It's all right for you, you're used to this!" I hissed. "For 'The Educated Gladiator' this is kitten's play."

"My eyes are weak," he sighed. "I have trouble seeing much these days."

"Listen!" I said. "I think it's about to begin."

What words were said, I cannot tell – but this kind of show is the same in every land. The crowd threw money into a pot, the drums began to beat and they ordered us to get ready.

On the other side of the circle, all of the fighters wore blue collars. A grey Nomat chief stalked along line of blues. At his side was a lioness on a long leash. It seemed well trained for it trotted along obediently after its master.

"What's he got there?" I said in a half hiss. Although we Kitons are known for our bravery, I didn't fancy going up against anything wild.

"Probably a pet. The lion is sacred to many of the tribes of the Kushionites. It represents their god Apurdemak."

You could always count on Spitulus for an answer. Where in Paws name did he learn this stuff?

At last, the grey whiskered chief chose his biggest fighter, a fierce cat with a palm leaf on his collar.

Our Nomat master was pleased with his rival's choice and now it was his turn. As he padded down our line I felt my breath inside my head. He passed the two newcomers and stopped right in front of us – eying me and Spitulus.

Spitulus was the biggest cat on our side, or on either side. With a smile, the Nomat tapped him on the nose. The blue leader snarled when he saw this and they chattered away in their own tongue. It ended with nods. A second blue fighter sprang into the circle.

"That's not fair," I spat. "That's two against one."

"Tell Haireena I'm sorry," said Spitulus, rubbing his eyes. They armed him with a long spear and he padded slowly into the circle.

I suppose I should have been glad. My rival did have a weakness after all. He was bigger than me, richer than me, wiser than me, but half blind. Poor

Spitulus would be no match for the two blues. They'd stay out of his reach, torment him til he grew weak, and bring him down like hunters after an elephant or some other great beast.

"Tell her yourself!" I shouted springing into the ring beside the giant. I was still tied to my stake by the leash. No one in the crowd gasped. One nomat got up and went to buy drinks from a passing water seller. A drummer followed him. "Drumming must be thirsty work," I thought.

The blue side were not happy. A jabbering exchange followed.

"Go and sit down, I beg!" said Spitulus. "Don't do this."

"It is done," I laughed as our two opponents padded towards us.

The first of the fighters had a dagger and a golden helmet. The second of the blues had a three-pointed trident. Spitulus was armed with his spear. I had no weapon.

The blues split up and made their way around the circle towards us.

"Look out Spitulus!" I cried. "They're coming."

"Even I can see that," hissed the giant.

The fighter in the helmet sprang at me, dagger in paw. He was big but he was slow. I rolled aside and he hit the dust with a groan. I noticed the strange shape of his golden helmet, now dented and covered in dust.

"He's got a hat shaped like a fish," I shouted. "Looks like a flat fish now!" I added.

"Interesting," said Spitulus, sticking out a great paw and blocking a glancing blow with his spear. "The Purmillo fights with a dagger and wears a fish shaped helmet. He represents the fish."

There was a crack and a groan. I glanced back.

"Traditionally, the Purmillo fights against Petiarius – the fisher..."

Spitulus's words were lost in the crash of spear against blade. By now, my attacker had risen from the dust. He took off the dented helmet and threw it at my face. I ducked too late and it caught me on the side of the head. I let out a cry of pain.

"The fisher carries a trident, which is of course a special kind of fishing spear..." continued Spitulus.

I wasn't sure if I'd live to hear the end of this speech as my attacker came at me with the dagger.

The drummer had returned from the water seller and she began to strike up a beat. I remembered my training and began to move. The blow nearly connected, but the blade slashed at thin air. Twisting, I got a paw on his throat and then rolled him. He hissed as his knife fell to the sand.

"... so it is a fight between a fisher and a fish!" laughed Spitulus.

Somehow he'd got the trident off his attacker. The blue was crouching in the dust, as Spitulus carried on with his lecture.

"A fisher verses the fish. It's a sort of Roman joke, you see," he said, warming to his theme.

"Look out Spitulus! He's got a net!" I cried. As the words left my mouth, the blue lunged towards Spitulus and threw the net, trying to snare him.

Hearing my warning, Spitulus sprang sideways, clawed at the net and reeled his attacker in. Then he flung him net and all at the second blue.

Our Nomat master spat his approval. The reds cheered.

The two blues struggled and thrashed, but it was useless, they were entangled in a heap.

Spitulus leant on his spear waiting for a sign. Our master brought a claw across his own neck, the sign of the jugulare which means 'death' in any language.

The leader of the blues looked at his two tangled fighters and hissed. Clearly he thought that they could have done better. He patted his lioness on the head.

"What would he have me do?" asked Spitulus.

The answer was 'death' but Spitulus didn't see it.

I picked up the dented helmet from the sand.

"There's been enough killing," I said. Then I turned and threw the helmet as hard as I could at the lioness. It struck the beast in the eye and it snarled. There were cries as it turned on its cruel master and leapt into the crowd.

"Run!" I cried.

The 'Educated Gladiator' stood rooted to the spot.

"Are you sure?" he hissed. "Couldn't we wait for a better time?"

"This is a great time!" I replied.

The lioness had let go of its master. But his wife was prodding at it with a long spear. Snarls filled the air and the crowd started to panic.

I sprang across to the far side of the circle, with Spitulus at my tail. In a few bounds he'd overtaken me. A crowd had suddenly appeared. Perhaps an escaped lion was more exciting than gladiators or maybe the snake show had finished?

"What about Haireena?" I called. "We can't leave her."

Spitulus had forgotten about his translator.

"Forgive me!" he cried, slowing to a walk. "You are right. Perhaps the Master has her?"

We doubled back to the camp and the red sun was sinking as we approached our group of tents.

"Here," said Spitulus, passing me a long dagger.

"Where did you get that?" I asked.

"I took it from one of the blue faces in the ring," he replied.

I wondered about Spitulus. He'd said that he couldn't see, but he didn't have much trouble spotting foes in the arena. I wondered whether it was his nerves, or his eyes – that were the problem.

As we came to the biggest tent in the camp, Spitulus told me to wait for his signal. I made ready with the blade.

"Will it be guarded?," I whispered.

He nodded. "Prepare yourself," he growled.

I let out a warlike hiss as we crashed in nose-first. Spitulus laughed, for the tent was empty.

"How did you know?" I asked.

"They must be out looking for us," he answered.

Inside we found a colourful doorway decorated with a lion, stitched in golden thread. Spitulus made the signal for silence, and then nodded to me to enter. But I shook my head.

"Not this time," I whispered. "You go first!"

The gladiator pushed his nose through the door and I heard a great thud. A wooden table crashed to the floor and pinned him by the tail.

"I'm sorry!" gasped a voice.

"Haireena," I cried, full of joy. She stood before me exactly as I had remembered. Her great amber eyes beamed like the moon.

"By Mighty Klaws," moaned Spitulus licking his tail. "You have a strong arm on you Haireena! I've seen lesser blows end bouts in the arena."

"Forgive me!" she said. "I thought the Master had come back. I heard cries but I didn't dare look."

"Haireena! You're safe. It's er... good to see you again," I muttered.

"What now?" asked Spitulus, licking his wounds. "We are not yet free. I daren't guess what the Emperor will do to us if we return without his prize."

"Is this the great gladiator that the songs tell of?"

"You sound as if you have given up," said Haireena.

She had a point. But I'm not the type to kick a cat when he's down.

"Let's go!" I said, springing to the door.

"Wait! We can't go without my vase," said Haireena.

It did cross my mind that although we'd just saved Haireena from a life as a Nomat's slave, she now wanted us to risk our lives for her shopping. My tail began to flick. Haireena shot me a dark look.

"How come you females always know what I'm thinking?" I moaned.

"That's not so hard with you," she laughed.

I looked at Spitulus. I wasn't sure about this.

"She's right. We need that vase to guide us."

"Alright! We will find this thing you seek," I sighed. "What are we looking for?"

As usual, Spitulus was ready with the details.

"It is a tall vase made of a shiny black stone called amunite that is only found in this land. There are a series of small holes, set around the rim."

"Be careful!" said Haireena. "It will be guarded."

"Don't worry – we're not scared of a few Nomats, are we Spitulus?"

"Do not underestimate the Nomats," said Spitulus. Once they ruled their river kingdom as well as the great kingdom of Misr or 'Fleagypt' as you call it. What this band is doing here, I am not sure. I had not heard that they preyed on travellers either."

"I didn't know they taught history at gladiator school..." I began.

"I taught myself," said the giant. "As one must – except those born to the purple cushion."

"Well that's all very interesting. Now by Woool's Balls, can we leave this place?"

It was decided that Spitulus would overpower the guards and take the vase, whilst Haireena would steal some camels.

"Shall I go with you Haireena. It'll be safer," I offered.

"No thanks," she replied, picking up a bundle from the corner. It was a bow, smaller than the ones in our land, and a quiver of arrows.

"You can get us a frog."

"Fetch a frog?" I hissed in amazement, starting to bristle.

"Let me explain..." began Spitulus.

"Haireena – I know that our first date did not go well. But do not mock me. I have journeyed across sea and sand to be with you."

"In these lands, no one would dream of going on an expedition without a frog. You must find one," said Haireena seriously.

"Unless you would prefer to overpower the guards and take the vase or steal the camels?" added Spitulus.

"Ridiculous!" I cried. "Anyway, I expect your croaking friend is in a cooking pot by now."

"There is no fear of that," began Spitulus. "The sages of this land write that frogs have long been sacred to the Kushionites..."

Rather than hear the end of this lecture, I nodded.

"Where should I look?" I muttered.

"Near water," she said. "Call him and you'll see."

It was dark as I crept from the tent and followed my nose towards the river. I was a little wounded that Haireena didn't need me with her.

I listened for Nomats but I heard nothing. Perhaps they were searching the streets of Catage for us?

"Sent to find a frog!" I muttered to myself.

I walked for hours. The path led me to a field full of tall grass – at least three tails high. It was a surprise to find such a plant growing after the dusty wastes of the desert.

Later, Spitulus told me that I'd been walking through a field of sorgum grass – a sacred plant in the land of Kush. Like my father, Spitulus seemed to know the answer to absolutely everything. Unlike my father, it was probably the right answer rather than something he'd picked up from a cart driver's wife at the fish stall. I did miss father though. My thoughts ran to where he was, and what he was doing. Worrying about me, or his money, no doubt.

When I found the river I gave a silent mew of delight. Looking around to check that there were no Nomats lurking, I was ready to search for signs of a frog. This is hard as frogs leave no signs.

I decided to look under stones, but there were no stones. I decided to look under logs, but there were no logs. There was only the wide water and the mud that covered everything like a brown watery desert.

I found no frogs, but I got the feeling that something was waiting in the water. I felt its eyes on me.

A little ripple broke the stillness and something moved on the bank. It was a frog at last! Alright – I admit that it was a small one. I worried about whether it would be good enough for Haireena. I decided to stalk it anyway.

Back at school I was an excellent stalker. I would have won the stalking competition in my year if Howl hadn't brought his own shrubbery to the final. However, I was finding it almost impossible to follow this creature without being spotted. There were no good places to hide. What I would have given for a decent tree or even a fallen log to lurk behind. The only thing giving any cover at all was a bed of reeds running along the bank. I didn't fancy getting my paws wet but it was the only way to get myself within pouncing distance.

I thought of Haireena as I took my first step. I had to do it for her. The water was surprisingly warm as my paws sank into the silt.

My prey leapt from reed to reed. Its feet must have been incredibly sticky, in order to cling on like that. I shadowed it carefully, like a true hunter. The true hunter makes no sound. The first that the prey knows of the true hunter is when he goes for the kill. Well, in this case I wasn't going to kill it, just get it into a bag. I hid behind a large reed clump and waited. One more hop and it would be mine.

There was a sudden splash and something knocked into me at speed. My footing gone, I was thrown into the reeds. A dark shape filled the river before me. An enormous mouth loomed through the foam, packed with cruel teeth. The thing let out a dreadful bellow and its leathery mouth snapped for my throat. But its jaws would not close – they were caught on the shaft of an arrow. Then the water turned red as two more arrows hissed into the monster's mouth.

"Who taught you to use a bow like that?" I asked as I shook myself dry in front of the small fire.

"My father," laughed Haireena.

"The fish seller?" I said in amazement. "I didn't see crocodile meat for sale at his stall."

"He was not always a fish seller," she answered. "Before we came to Rome he was an archer in the Queen's guard."

"I hope to thank him one day," I said. "But there's no need to risk a fire. I'm damp but ready to go now."

"The fire is not for you," said Haireena. "If the bow is put away when damp, it will snap."

"I see," I said. My pride was a little hurt.

As soon as it was dry, Haireena packed the bow away in its little leather bag.

I must admit to feeling secretly pleased when Spitulus told me that he hadn't managed to find the vase. At least we had both failed in our tasks.

Haireena had done well. She'd sneaked back to the Nomats camp and stolen us two fine camels. These beasts were much larger than my last one. Poor Misis! She wasn't fit for such a cruel journey. These two had darker coats and looked ready for anything that our trip through the sands would bring.

"Well done!" I laughed. "What are we going to call them?"

"We never give our beasts names," said Haireena. "Never get too close to your animal, for who knows what dangers the road may bring?"

"Shall I fill the water skins?" I asked as Haireena sprang onto her camel.

Haireena nodded. Peering into the water, I caught a smell on the wind.

"Nomats," I hissed, sniffing the breeze. "I'd almost forgotten about them."

"They have not forgotten us," warned Spitulus. "Hunting down escaped slaves is like a sport in this land. They even invite other tribes to join the hunt."

I wondered what books he got this knowledge from – but this was not the time to ask.

"Which way then?" I asked.

"We'll keep a little way away from the river," said Haireena. "Perhaps the Nomats won't follow us through this swamp."

AUGUSTPUSS XXV

August 25th

A Lucky Spin

Today, another riddle was answered.

"Why were we following the ship with red sails?" asked Eddipuss.

"Red sails means it's a trade ship – bound for Fleagypt, " said the Mate.

"Why not look for another ship on the trade route and follow it to port?" asked Eddi.

"Why not?" hissed the Mate. "By the Titan's tail – what do you think we've been doing all this time? Now we only have five day's fresh water."

"How can we be lost?" asked Jebel. "With a fine pot to guide us?"

Soon we were all sat around the fire in the galley. The Mate gave the pot a spin and just as before, strange pictures began to flicker on the walls.

We saw ancient tombs. Hooded soldiers in rows charged against each other, and at last, a great king came, with a snarling leopard at his feet.

The moving pictures were so much like life that Eddipuss hid his face with his paws. The strangest figure seemed to float behind the king. In its paw was a long pole, like the shaft of a spear. But instead of a tip, the spear ended in a feather.

"What's that thing?" I asked.

"That's Victory of course," said Jebel. "Look at him touching the king with his lucky feather!"

"I don't like it! Make it stop!" cried Eddipuss.

"Can it tell us where to sail?" I asked.

The moving pictures on the wall turned to stars.

"Look!" said Jebel.

"It's a map," said Eddi in excitement.

"What a shame it is on the wall!" I moaned. "For if only we had it in our paw it could be of great use."

"Have you two got fur for brains?" hissed the Mate. "You can see the stars, so mark their positions on a map. Then line us up with them and sail in that direction."

"I see. That is how it is done," I said sheepishly.

"Ginger squab!" muttered the Mate.

"When will we make port in the land of Kush?" I asked, changing the subject.

"Never," growled the Mate. "It has no ports."

"It has a river," said Jebel. "We must sail up it."

"What about your mistress and her treasure?" asked Eddipuss. "Tell us about that cavern. Is it really piled with gold, as you said?"

The Mate let out a low hiss.

"Seek not The Fur of the Gods," he growled. Then he stalked out of the galley in a rage.

"The Fur of the Gods? What in the name of the Gorgan's Goat does that mean?" asked Eddi.

THE SECRET DIARY OF S.O.S.

Day XV

"These fish taste sweet," I said, tucking into a fat trout. "The Kushionites are lucky to have treats like this on their doorstep."

"The ancients could not eat fish," laughed Spitulus. "Their gods forbid it. However, it would seem that our Nomat friends do not follow that law."

"You're making that up," I laughed. "How can you know that?"

"There are pictures on their tombs..." began Spitulus.

A sudden stab of pain in my flank made me cry out. I sprang up and rolled around in the mud to shake off the creature's hold. But I rolled too far down the bank and hit the water with a splash.

"Got him!" I laughed, dragging myself back up the bank. "A drowned mosquito is better than a live one.

"I fear that your enemy outnumbers you," said Spitulus pointing at a cloud of insects which were following me up the bank.

"Look at the size of them," I cried, backing away.

"Silence!" hissed Haireena. "Do you think the Nomats have no ears?"

"Sorry!" I said in a tone that made it clear that I wasn't sorry. "I expect they've gone back to their sands anyway," I said. They're a desert tribe after all.

I shouldn't think they'd like to hang around here in the capital of the Mosquito Empire."

Even as the words left my mouth I knew that I was saying something foolish. Am I under some spell that makes me say the most stupid things when I am around Haireena?

Spitulus was already shaking his head.

"Without the river, the Nomats would all be dead. Have you noticed it rain in this land? The flood surge comes down the river from far away and that's what makes the soil so fertile."

"Anything else you'd like to add pawfessor?" I asked.

Before he could answer, Haireena let out a hiss.

"Quiet!" she whispered. "We are discovered."

A cloud of brown dust filled the horizon.

"Is that a storm?" I asked.

"Nomats," said Haireena. "Travelling at speed. The wind blows their dust before them."

"We must go," she cried leaping onto her camel. The beast let out a moan and she whispered in its ear. She hadn't given the two new camels names. She was probably right after what had happened to my poor Misis. Spitulus sprang onto his ride and I got up behind Haireena.

"Fly!" she cried, pulling at the reins – and the beast shot off like an arrow from the bow.

We broke from the marshlands and headed for harder ground. Now the camels could really run. The beasts got into their stride but I must admit that it was all I could to do cling on behind Haireena. Spitulus had the bigger camel but he began to fall behind and we had to check our speed to keep him in sight.

"Hurry Spitulus! They're close," she called.

"Where did you learn to ride like this?" I asked.

But my voice was lost in the rush of wind and the beat of hooves on the stones. Knowing Haireena, I expect her grandfather was a royal camel racer or something.

After three hours we came to a patch of trees on a slight rise – the nearest thing to a hill that I'd seen in this flat land.

We got off the camels and let them rest. They soon followed their noses to a hidden water hole at the base of the hill.

From the top of the rise I saw what looked like a large house with a flat roof. It was so big that it filled the sky.

"Are we stopping ?" I asked. "That big house looks like it would make a good place to stay the night."

"If you like sleeping with the dead," laughed Haireena.

I gave her a puzzled look.

"It's a Purramid, an ancient tomb," said Spitulus.

"Are you sure? It's made of mud. And it doesn't look much like the ones I've seen," I said. "The top's been flattened."

"In my country, they are build of mud brick, and

they have flat tops," said Haireena.

"I didn't know the Kushionites had them too," I said.

"We had them first," said Haireena.

"She may be right about that. Although the wise have much to say on the subject..." began Spitulus. But before he could continue, Haireena pointed out a cloud of dust, which was just visible on the horizon. I thought I saw flashes of gold from within it, but it could have been the sun playing tricks on my weary eyes.

"Our friends don't sleep," I said walking towards the camels. "Shall we go?"

"A moment more. We need to stay long enough for the animals to drink," said Haireena.

Camels are big drinkers, apparently.

"Good!" said Spitulus. "I'm going to take a look at the tomb. Haireena – will you bring the camels once they have had their fill?"

I thought about staying with Haireena, but I didn't want to risk another rejection. She'd probably only order me to brush the camels. So instead, I followed behind Spitulus as he lumbered down the slope towards the great building.

As we got closer, I saw that the tomb was made of thousands of tiny mud bricks. At the base stood a statue of a lion-god. His outstreached paw was pointing straight into the nameless desert.

"Who's that?" I asked.

"Apedakmat," said Spitulus. "You'll find him all through this land, and sometimes in Misr too."

The gladiator circled for a moment and began to flick his tail, as he did when he was deep in thought.

"Fascinating," he purred, his tail swished.

"There's nothing like a big old tomb to take your mind off a horde of Nomats " I said.

I was about to tell him to get going, unless he wanted to get a really good look inside a tomb. But we Kitons don't run from a challenge, so I kept my mouth shut. Then I noticed some wobbly writing.

"Is that the language of the Kushionites?" I asked. "What does it say?"

"It is an ancient tongue," said Spitulus, rubbing the sand out of the cracks. "A language of picture-words. Few can read these glyphs now..."

"Nevermind," I said spotting Haireena racing her camel towards us at full tilt.

"Luckily, I am one of the few who can now read them," said Spitulus. "It says: 'Seek not the Fur of the Gods!' and by that it means..."

"Enough Spitulus!" I shouted. "We must go!"

Haireena was charging down the hill with the reins to Spitulus' camel in her left paw. The unmistakable shape of a camel and rider appeared on top of the hill behind her. This first rider was followed by another, and then more.

I sprang up to take my place behind Haireena. But she was riding so fast that I lost my hold and I was thrown into the dust. I rolled three times and ended up at the base of the statue.

I called out to her but she didn't stop. She'd left me behind for the Nomats. This was hard to bear!

By now Haireena and Spitulus were some way down the track. A stream of black-clothed riders were swarming down the hill towards me.

A part of me wished they would take me, if Haireena wouldn't.

"Spitulus! Wait!" I called.

His camel slowed to a stop and to my relief, the big gladiator rode back for me.

"Admiring the statues?" said Spitulus, pausing for a moment to examine the pointing lion.

We charged off down the track. I thought that my camel was running before – but now we were flying down the road.

I looked back to see the swarm of dark-robed riders falling back.

"I don't think they're gaining," I said.

"If Fortune wills it, they'll need to water their beasts soon," called Spitulus.

Two hours down the road we came to row upon row of huts made of mud brick. It was quiet as a Purramid, with no living thing in sight. Not even a Nomat.

Spitulus and I rested while Haireena, who was the fastest rider, doubled back to look for signs of them.

I padded into one of the huts. It was a lonely place,

empty apart from a few scorched cooking stones and a broken pot.

"Nobody at home," I said. "Where did they go?"

I wondered what terrible event might make a whole town disappear. Was it a war? Or a raging storm or famine that had left it in this state?

"The workers who built the Purramid lived in this town. When it was done, their task was finished so they left."

"I wonder where they all went?" I asked, thinking back to the flat-topped tomb. It was big but this empty town was bigger still. All this work for a dead king's house.

Then I noticed a hut with a statue of the lion god outside.

"Him again," I said.

"You noticed him too?" asked Spitulus.

"What did the words on the Purramid mean?" I asked. "You were going to translate for me."

"Seek not The Fur of the Gods," said Spitulus. "The ancients believed that the Gods were covered in fur made of thin strands of the finest gold. They also thought their bones were made of precious stones."

"So it's a warning?" I asked.

"Yes!" laughed Spitulus. "To scare off treasure hunters. The ancients spoke of all the treasures they had taken from the Furroahs. Some believe the gold was cursed, and that the Queen of Kush buried it a cavern at the source of the Nile."

With a swish, a shadow swept into the hut. The shadow had been eavesdropping on our conversation.

"We're nowhere near the source of the Nile," laughed Haireena. "We must be fifty miles or more from the river. Besides, every kitten knows that Mother Nile flows right through the land of Kush and onwards. Where it ends, no tongue can tell."

Now I understood – the Emperor had sent Spitulus on a treasure hunt. Haireena had been taken along to translate, but she'd fallen in love with her homeland. She didn't need me to rescue her. There was a fondness in the way she spoke to Spitulus. It was hard for me to hear it.

"The course of a river may change over the ages," said Spitulus, as he sprang out into the sun.

"Any sign of our Nomat friends?" he asked.

"No sign," said Haireena. "But just because a thing cannot be seen, it doesn't mean it's not there."

"What?" I said.

Spitulus leapt up onto his camel and turned the beast around so it was facing down the road we'd came on.

"Er, aren't we headed the wrong way?" I asked.

"We're going back," said Spitulus. "Perhaps we will find the answer inside that Purramid."

AUGUSTPUSS XXVII

August 27th

As the days pass, we follow the stars. Two nights ago, the sea turned into the mouth of a great river, just as Jebel had said it would. We were all glad of the fresh water – none more than the frog. He leapt for joy, right out of the boat and into the river so we had to get a bucket and haul him on board.

AUGUSTPUSS XXVIII

August 28th

This morning the river opened out into a land of marshes. There are plenty of fish and black crabs to eat. Jebel is always trying to sit on my cushion. Although he is clean for a frog, I fear he may stain it.

Each night we spin the pot and set our course by the stars. I cannot get used to the strange pictures. Last night there was a god with the head like a lion. It stood next to another god with the head of a sheep. These two hold up the sky between them. I have often wondered why the gods should have different heads to the rest of us. Still there is something rather soft and comfortable about the idea of a sheep god with a nice warm fleece. I've decided to make him an offering so I've added him to my list of favourites.

AUGUSTPUSS XXIX

August 29th

Today I thought my new sheep god had answered our prayers. The marsh opened out into a deep river. But our good fortune did not last for long. I was dozing on deck when Eddipuss shouted: "Rocks!"

I sprang to the rail and looked out on a terrible scene. The river was flecked with points of white. I heard a grinding scrape and the Mate began to shout.

"By Neptune's pointed fork! Turn her about! We can't sail through rocks!"

The Mate and I worked the oars while Eddipuss steered for the far side of the channel. The currents gave us a good battle, and many times we were dragged back. After two hard hours, we reached the safety of the bank and tied up our craft.

"What now?" asked Eddi. "The stars are leading us away from the boat."

"I can't take you any further," said the Mate, pacing in a sad circle around the cushion where Jebel sat. "Please. Seek not the Fur of the Gods," he muttered, his voice trailing away in a half-hiss.

"What do you mean by that?" asked Eddi.

"Gold!" said the Mate sadly. "It'll be your ruin."

"His son is in prison. That's why he needs gold," explained Eddipuss.

"So you're true treasure seekers then?" said the Mate. "You'd better get going then."

THE SECRET DIARY OF S.O.S.

Day XVII

I don't know who I am writing this diary for. I started off writing it for Haireena, but now I'm not so sure. I'd write it for myself but I'm not much of a reader. I'll carry on with it, as there is little else to do.

As I take up the pen in my paw, I'm sitting in the darkness, waiting for danger to pass. Yesterday, we rode all day to escape the Nomats. Today we rode all day back towards them! Spitulus says the Purramid where they attacked us is 'interesting' and that is good enough for Haireena.

So we rode back through the sands and through the empty town until at last we saw the Purramid looming in the dawn. A patch of green on the hill marked the water hole. Our thirsty camels found it soon enough. When it was my turn to drink, I lapped the water straight down. Spitulus drank slowly, and then we made our way down the hill to the statue of the lion.

I noticed something unusual about the statue. The Lion God was looking at the Purramid, but his arm was pointing straight out into the desert.

"Hey Spitulus. What he's pointing at?" I asked.

'The Educated Gladiator' didn't answer. He was lost in his own thoughts, studying the writing at the base of the tomb.

I decided to have a look for myself. I padded out into the sands for a while and sniffed around a bit.

"Do not wander off!" warned Haireena. "There may be Nomats near."

"We Kitons are known for our courage in battle..." I began. But she was probably right. Besides, I fancied another drink. On the way back, I noticed something dark sticking out of the sand. I scraped away at the sand with my paw and uncovered a straight line. So I dug out another pawful and a shape began to appear.

"Spitulus," I called. "Look at this!"

He didn't answer so I decided to go on.

I've always loved digging. I can do it for hours. I was one of the best diggers in my school. I came second in my whole year. I would have been first if Gnawus hadn't brought a secret shovel into the final.

Digging in the sand is easy compared to digging in the mud of the Land of the Kitons. Although you've got to watch it as the sand gets can get in between your pads, which is no laughing matter. In two minutes my line had opened out into a shaft.

Back at home, any digging competition is judged by the size of your soil mound. I'm not boasting when I say that I had a very impressive mound. But in this land it's not the mound that counts, it's what's underground. By the time Haireena had joined me, I'd uncovered a large square door under the sand.

"An entrance!" cried Haireena. I hadn't heard her sound this excited since our date in the Golden House. Actually she was more excited now than she was then.

The secret entrance was guarded by two statues. One was our friend the Lion God again, and the other was rather odd. It was a Sheep God. When I saw this, I tried hard not to laugh. What fool would want to worship a sheep for Peus' sake!

"Spitulus! Come!" shouted Haireena. "He's made a discovery."

I looked up from my digging to see Spitulus racing towards us. "When she calls, he comes running," I sighed. Then, I decided that I perhaps I wasn't being fair. He was probably excited about my 'find' as we diggers like to call the things that we find under the sand. But the sweet pride of discovery soon turned bitter.

"Nomats!" he hissed.

"Look," I said, wiping the sand from the bottom of one of the statues. "What can this mean?"

Haireena looked at the writing and translated it:

"Take the Great Lion by the tail and Amun by the horns."

"Another puzzle," I moaned.

A number of horns began to blow in the distance.

"I think the Nomats may have banded together, in a hunting party," said Spitulus.

"What are they hunting? Not desert foxes, surely?" I said. Then I realised that I'd done it again. There was something about being with Haireena that made me ask the most stupid questions. The Nomats were hunting us.

All this time Spitulus was staring at the statues.

"That one must be Lord Ram..." he said, patting the sheep by the horns. I tried hard not to laugh, but can you blame me?

"...and this one is the Great Lion," said Spitulus "But it makes no sense. How can I take the lion by the tail? He does not have a tail!"

The horns sounded again. Drums and answered it from the direction of the hill.

"Try this!" I cried grabbing hold of the horns and hanging on to the stump where the lion god's tail was once attached.

I gave it an enormous heave. Nothing happened.

"You've provided the brains today," laughed Spitulus. "So I'll provide the muscle."

The gladiator pulled at the two statues with all his strength. The ground began to shake and with a rumble a dark hole appeared in the sand. When the dust had settled, we stood before a wide set of stone steps leading down to a cave below.

The camels grumbled and spat as we took them by their ropes and led them down.

"I told you we should have given them names," I said.

Haireena whispered something in their ears and they followed us into the darkness.

"How do we close it?" I hissed. Before the words had left my mouth there was a grinding rumble and the stone doors slammed shut behind us.

It was completely dark apart from a shaft of light coming from the end of the tunnel. As we moved onwards, the corridor opened out into a larger space with stone steps.

"Why make it so wide?" I asked.

"For the procession," said Spitulus. "When the the king went into the next world, he did not travel light. They had to carry his posessions in by the cart load."

We padded carefully downwards. A flash tore through the dark. Haireena had got a torch lit. The hall where we stood had a high roof and a line of huge statues loomed through the dark.

"Gods from Misr!" cried Spitulus. "Moth, and Pawrus of the Underworld. How did they get here? A present from the Furroahs perhaps?"

"You forget that our tribes once ruled the land you call 'Fleagypt'" said Haireena. "There was a time when we were the masters. Then they invaded and enslaved us. Now Rome rules their land and there is peace."

I looked at Haireena. So beautiful, and wise too.

"Come!" called Spitulus. He'd discovered a narrow set of steps leading up past the heads of the statues. A few leaps led us to a gap in the stones.

"I'm too big for this!" said Spitulus. "Can either of you squeeze through?"

I sprang to the crack and began to crawl down the tunnel. Soon I could taste fresh air – it felt good after the stuffy air of the tomb.

I padded out into the sunlight and found myself on a high ledge on the outside of the Purramid. The wind howled across the stones.

Far below I saw the Nomats spreading out to search the base of the Purramid. I wondered what the punishment for breaking into a tomb would be?

Not waiting to find out, I padded back to tell the others what I'd seen.

"We'll stay here till nightfall, and then try to slip away unseen," said Haireena. We Kitons are known for our courage – but I liked the sound of her plan.

"You may need this," said Spitulus, passing down a wooden chest. It slipped from his paws and the old wood split on the stone floor. A flower of dust bloomed in the torchlight.

"Treasure?" I coughed.

"Weapons," corrected Spitulus. He took a sword for himself and threw me a trident. Haireena took a longer bow. With it came a quiver made of copper containing arrows with coloured tips.

"Where next?" I asked.

"Look up there," purred Spitulus in excitement. "What do you see?"

Apurdemak, the Lion God was the third statue in the group. The stone giant stood with his paw outstretched.

"I have an idea..." began Spitulus.

"Don't tell me," I said. "I already know. We're going to head where the statue is pointing. Right?"

SEPTEMBER I

September 1st

It is now four days since we left the ship and walked off in search of the treasure. We've found nothing, only swarms of vicious dark flies. When they bite, they stay in your skin until they are full of your blood.

Yesterday we felt the ground beneath our pads get firmer. Eddi and I were pleased but Jebel begged us to fill up the water skins. A desert is no place for a frog.

We passed on into the wilds, seeing few signs of life. The odd snake left tracks in the sand. On the fifth day we came to a city of raised mounds. Small white pebbles were scattered around each of them.

"Where is everyone?" asked Eddipuss. "Why go to the bother of making all of this and just leave it?"

I made no answer – for I'd seen similar places in my homeland.

"Look!" said Eddipuss. "A hole! Let's have a dig down there, we might find some treasure."

Jebel and I begged him to stop, but he wouldn't listen. An hour later, he emerged from the hole with nothing in his paws but dust.

"Go on then, ask me what I found," he moaned.

But we did not have to ask. The hole was empty save for a pile of bones, with its paws over its eyes.

"We must go," said Jebel.

So we span the pot again and got on our way.

Tonight I shall say a prayer to Fortune for I fear that we'll need her. Eddipuss should not have dug in that pit. I wish that I had stopped him. Now I have the feeling that there are eyes watching us. We march with all possible speed away from that place.

SEPTEMBER II

September 2nd

We are all alone in the end. I awoke from a night of dark dreams to find Eddipuss has gone. There was no note – for he cannot write. He didn't take a water skin and his little bundle of things was still in its usual place by the cooking fire.

I looked all around for tracks but I fear that I am no tracker. I will look again in the morning. There is little choice but to spin the pot once more and walk wherever it may lead me. I have never been any good at last words, which is strange, for it is often said that 'practice makes purrfect'. I have had a fair amount of practice at last words. To my dear wife and son. Since I have no treasure to leave you, I will leave these words of warning from the Stroic philosopher Pawraelius:

> *'When everything is looking ill,*
> *and you fear that you are cursed,*
> *Don't pray all day or run away –*
> *you'll only make things worse.'*

THE SECRET DIARY OF S.O.S.

Day XVIII

Goodbye Haireena. Now you'll never read this. You didn't return my love but it doesn't matter. Spitulus says it's not my fault but he's wrong. I mocked the Gods of this place. Now I'd plead with any god if it would bring you back.

Where the Lion statue pointed, we'd decided to follow. After three days riding, I was sick of the heat.

"I've been baked enough in this land," I said. "Haireena, I'd give all the treasures of your ancestors for a good long drink."

But as usual, no one was listening to me. They were both staring into the distance.

"At last!" said Spitulus. "It's the fort."

To tell the truth, it didn't look anything like any fort that I've ever seen. In Rome they make their forts out of wood using careful plans. In the Land of the Kitons, we find a big hill and sharpen the ends of the biggest trees we can get hold of. But this fort looked like a cliff. A big red rock sticking out of the desert like the crest on a newt.

"Jebel Barkal" whispered Haireena.

"Go on then. Please one of you tell me. What's Gerbil Baker when it's at home?" I sighed.

"Jebel Barkal," corrected Haireena.

"It's the ancient fortress of the Kushionites," said

Spitulus. "They think it looks like a sacred snake."

"A rearing cobra," corrected Haireena.

"Well a snake god is better than a sheep god!" I thought. But I kept this thought to myself. For I'd decided that if I was to have any chance of impressing Haireena, I needed to keep my mouth closed.

"This used to be the stronghold of the Kushionites. It fell into ruin many years ago," she explained.

"Is the treasure cave inside there?" I asked, already forgetting my new rule. Nobody answered me.

It was an hour's ride to the base of the cliff – and the camels were thirsty when we arrived. They made straight for a heap of old stones.

"It's a well!" I cried.

I found that the rope was still attached and I drew up the bucket.

"Drink your fill everyone," I said. "And top up your water skins while you're at it."

"Stop!" said Haireena. "Don't drink, I beg you! Spit it out!"

Luckily I'm a good spitter. I came fifth in my year at hissing and spitting. I was only out spat by the Gobbus twins – and drool runs in that family."

I spat out the mouthful without swallowing it.

"The wells here were poisoned after the last battle. It is not safe to drink," said Haireena.

"It tasted all right to me," I said. But before I could argue the case, something hissed through the air in front of me and bounced off the rim of the well.

"Don't even say it!" I moaned.

"Nomats!" hissed Spitulus.

We sprang after Haireena, who was already making her way towards the cliff face. As we ran, more arrows whizzed over our heads.

"Jebel Barkel was known for its winding stairs," said Spitulus.

"There!" said Haireena. She led us to a set of steps, cut into the red rock of the cliff.

"Are you sure?" I say, as we ran up the stairs. "I mean, I don't like to be cornered."

"Would you rather fight the Nomats in the open?" asked Spitulus.

"This Fort was built to be defended for weeks on end," said Haireena. "With luck, it'll keep us safe."

The climb was steep. As we turned a corner in the rock, I heard excited shouts below us. There was the tell-tale hiss again. This time Haireena got her bow out of the case and strung up an arrow. It flew straight and I heard a cry. Then Haireena screamed in pain.

"Are you hurt?" called Spitulus.

"Just a cut. My bow string snapped," she said.

The three of us tore up another set of steps and took cover by the base of a stone statue. It was the sheep god again. They do like their sheep in this land. Spitulus started to examine it.

"This is no time for that!" I cried.

"Spitulus stopped studying the writing and began to push at the sheep god's face with his head.

"Help me!" he said.

We sprang to the task and soon the great statue began to rock on its base. With a final heave we sent it crashing down the stone steps. When the dust had cleared, the path behind us was blocked.

"Hail Lord Ram!" I said, bowing before the statue's broken head "Baa! Sorry I didn't believe in you."

"Do not mock the gods of this place," said Spitulus. His expression was serious. "The word 'Baa' is their word for 'soul' and only the priests could utter it. The punishment for speaking it aloud was death."

"You might be right," I said. "I'm sorry!"

We continued our climb up into the fortress. Haireena spotted a window, high on the cliff. At the foot there was a basket and a rope.

"Funny place to leave an empty basket," I said.

"The defenders would use it to get up to that tower," explained Spitulus. "But the rope's been cut."

"That would make the perfect hiding place," I said springing towards the bottom of the cliff. The red stone was smooth and it was hard to get a hold but I thought I could make it. "I'll climb up there with the rope and you tie it on to the basket."

"How would you pull me up, if you got to the top?" he asked. Spitulus is a strong climber – and in a few moments he had reached the little window.

"What took you so long?" I called as he lowered the rope. Then I saw Haireena lying there. I put a paw to her face, but she didn't answer. Then I put her in the basket and Spitulus pulled her up to the tower.

"What's wrong? Is she wounded!" I cried.

Spitulus searched her coat carefully checking for wounds or bites. Then he picked up her bow.

"Look!" he said, picking up the quiver. The copper gleamed in the dipping sun. "I have been a fool!"

"It's my fault," I moaned. "I should never have mocked her gods."

"Here is our answer," said Spitulus.

He held up the quiver. The copper was bright, except at the bottom. It was stained green where the arrowheads had touched the metal.

"Poisoned arrows," he said. "That's why the ancients kept them in a metal quiver. Haireena must have got scratched when her bowstring snapped."

At first, I didn't believe him.

I put my nose to yours, Haireena. The breathing was faint. Then I looked out into the dark.

"Is there a cure?" I asked. "Anything?"

Spitulus shook his head. "Who knows what they put on the tips. There are many poisonous things in the desert. I fear she will not last the night."

Sudden flashes racked across the stone window, filling the room with lights. I heard cries from below.

"Nomats!" I cried.

"Curse them!" hissed Spitulus unsheathing his huge claws. His eyes were burning. "They've brought us to this pass and now they'll pay for it."

He drew his sword and began to mutter words

over the blade. I'd had enough gods for today, so I just picked up the trident.

Lights swept past the window – brighter this time.

"What demon's fire have they got there?" I asked.

"The ancients made flames with metals dug from these rocks," said Spitulus. "Perhaps they mean to burn us out."

"Shall we?" I asked, pointing to the basket. Spitulus nodded. Why wait for death in this stone tower, when we could make them pay dearly for Haireena's life.

"We'll fall on them from the sky," I said getting into the basket. "Just like that Sun god of theirs. What's his name?"

"Amun," said Spitulus squeezing in next to me.

"Wait!" I said. "There's no room for us both. Send me down first."

Spitulus swung the basket over the ledge and began to lower it. Through the cracks I saw sparks. What mischief were they cooking up for us?

When the basket crashed to the ground, I stuck my head out into the light. Nothing could prepare me for what I saw next. A ragged old ginger came struggling around the corner, puffing and wheezing as if he was about to breath his last. In his paw, he was nursing a frog.

"Father?" I cried.

SEPTEMBER V

September 5th

Fortune, I am sorry. I promise never to doubt you again. You have answered my prayers and brought me back the treasure I value the most

I gave my son quite a fright. By the way he was holding his trident, he was surprised to see me.

"Father?" he cried. "In the name of Mighty Paws! Mewpiter and the rest! What are you doing here?"

"I could ask you the very same question," I replied, not liking his tone. "For Peus sake!" I cried. "How ever did you manage to get yourself thrown into Hades Row? It was an Empire of worry and woe! You'll never know what I've been through."

"What you've been through?" he answered, in a lecturing tone which some say sounds a little like my own. "You have no clue! You grey whiskers think you've lived, but you haven't seen anything."

"Is that so?" I said in a half hiss.

"You don't know what it's like for the young," he sulked. "I was imprisoned by the Emperor."

"So was I," I answered.

"I escaped from Rome's worst prison."

"So did I."

"I've sailed across the Mare at the most dangerous time. The sailors call it 'The Closed Sea.'"

"So have I."

"I've saved a half-blind companion from death."

"So have I."

"I've spun a magical pot and seen visions."

"So have I."

"I've risked my life trying to find a frog."

"So have I," I said, holding up Jebel as the proof. "My frog can talk," I added.

"I've been chased through the desert by Nomats."

"So have I."

"I've fought as a gladiator in an arena."

"So have I."

"I've risked my life for the one I love,"

"So have I," I hissed.

He paused for a moment. Had he come to the end of his list?

"For mother?" he asked.

"For you my son!" I answered.

It is rare for S.O.S. to run out of words, for he takes after his mother. I think he may have started again but we were interrupted by a voice from above.

"Who's there?" I hissed, jumping in fright.

"That's Spitulus," said my son. "He's a friend."

"Quickly," boomed the voice, so we both stepped into the basket.

As you readers have but one pair of eyes each, I will leave it to my son to tell the next part of the tale. Forgive him if his words are not as fine as mine, it is not for want of teaching. We've spent a lot on his education but he has only mastered the lyre.

165

THE DIARY OF S.O.S.

Day XX

I had many things to say to my father. In fact I could argue with him all day and night. If he'd sent the money to buy me out of prison, none of this would have happened. And why did he travel alone through Ostia with no guards to help him look after his money? That's what I want to know. But I decided to hold my tongue. This was no time for a family squabble.

Spitulus hauled the basket up with ease, and we were soon back in the tower. The big gladiator had tears in his eye. I remembered Haireena,

"She's gone," he whispered

She lay curled motionless in the corner.

"She's been poisoned," I explained.

"Now, I know I thing or two about poisons," began father.

"Don't start father!" I begged. "There's nothing anyone can do."

But my father is not a good listener.

"What would be the most poisonous beast in this desert? I have heard it said..."

"For Peus sake father! This is no time for one of your talks," I hissed. I threw myself down on the floor by Haireena and began to weep.

My father paid no heed and carried on rambling.

"I wonder what kind of poison they might find out

here. A snake perhaps, or some insect with a deadly sting?" he began.

I was about to shout at him to shut his mouth and give the dead some peace when something unexpected happened.

"I know," said a voice.

My father's frog was talking. In fact, I think he said something about it earlier but I guessed that he was babbling as usual.

Spitulus and I stared in amazement. My father didn't seem to see anything strange and he answered the frog as if he was chatting to a neighbour about the chariot races or the position of a scratching post.

"Jebel," began my father. I could tell he was starting to get irritated. "When we first met, you promised me that you were not poisonous?"

"My apologies," said the frog. "We don't like to tell everyone about it. It makes them nervous."

Spitulus smiled.

"That explains why frogs are sacred in this land," he said.

"Sacred indeed!" hissed my father. "Sacred to the archers of this land, no doubt."

I looked down at the frog in the bucket. It was strange to be talking to a frog, but I had a question.

"Is there anything we can do to cure Haireena?" I asked.

"Put her on the cushion," came the reply.

"By Mewpiter!" My father cried.

"I suppose it might work," he said. "It brought Jebel here back from the world beyond."

My first thought was that the burning sun must have turned my father's mind. In his case it wouldn't need much turning. Then I looked at the frog hopping happily in his bucket. Anything was worth a try.

Spitulus carefully lifted Haireena onto the cushion and set her down gently.

"The cushion was a present for your mother, but I don't suppose she'll want it now," said father. "It's covered in Peus knows what kind of stains."

We sat down and waited for whatever the dawn would bring. A few hours later there was a scratching in the dark. Then there was a hiss.

I couldn't believe what I was hearing.

"It's Haireena," whispered Spitulus. "I think she's breathing once again."

I sprang over to where she was on the cushion and tried to help her stand.

"Not yet," croaked a voice. "Wait for the dawn. Do not move her from the cushion until it is done."

"How can this be?" I asked.

Then I remembered that I sat with the two cats in the world most likely to be able to give an answer to an impossible question like that. Luckily Spitulus answered before my father.

"There is a legend about a Queen called Cleocatra," he said. "She was poisoned by her husband. Her favourite servant lay her down to sleep on a cushion, that had been given to her by a priestess. It brought her back to life.

"Cleocatra's Kushion?" my father whispered.

"There is more," he said sadly. But his tale was interupted by a familiar voice.

"Spitulus?" it called.

My heart leapt to hear Haireena speak, even though she wasn't calling my name.

"Are you well enough to walk?" asked the big gladiator. "We'll leave this place as soon as you're able."

"I think so," said Haireena, getting up from the cushion.

Ten minutes later we all stood on the path below the tower.

"Father, did you see the Nomats. When you made your way up here?" I asked.

"When we span the pot, they ran away from the lights," said father. "I'll explain it later."

"No need..." I began.

"They will be back in the daylight," said Spitulus. "Haireena is too weak to travel far."

The path up the fortress was winding and it was some hours before we reached the very top. We found a cleft that led inside and looked in awe. The whole mountain was hollow.

"Get her inside quickly," said Spitulus. "We must find a hiding place."

The day wore on slowly and Haireena rested on the

cushion, while we explored the tunnels carved into the mountain.

We found many rooms decorated with carvings. There were stone fountains, and statues all in rows with claws and teeth made of gold.

"Look at that father," I said. "You could dig those teeth out. They might be worth something."

My father looked at me in amazement.

"Spitulus. How long has that statue stood there?"

"Five hundred years, perhaps," said the giant. "Maybe more."

"Five hundred years," hissed my father. "And you would have me tear it to pieces would you? To fund some folly, like golden strings for your lyre."

Perhaps this was a bad time to tell him that I needed a new lyre as well as the strings. The Emperor hadn't given it back.

"Sorry!" I said. "I know you like your gold. Don't deny it. You're always talking about how much gold you will need for things."

"For you!" said my Father. "I wanted to give you a proper start in life. But now I think we are all be better off without it."

I looked at the statue and wondered if he was right. Perhaps I'd take up a cheaper instrument, like the drum.

On we walked through ancient halls. All the time Spitulus was examining everything he saw and making notes and drawings in his book. We found many precious things, but not a scrap to eat or drink, and no way out.

"Why did the ancients leave this place?" I asked, admiring the latest lot of statues. Having done a bit of masonry back at the Golden House, I could appreciate the craft that had gone into them.

"We'd better not speak of that," said Spitulus. "Something bad happened here. Jebel Barkal was abandoned soon after."

My father and I sat with Haireena while Spitulus explored the fortress.

In the dimming light, Spitulus rushed back in.

"Please don't say it!" I cried.

"The Nomats are back!" he hissed. "They are gathering under the cliff. We must shut the doors."

Together, we pushed against the great stone gates to our cave. Once closed, a wooden bar was slid across.

"That should hold them for a while," said Spitulus.

As darkness fell, I returned to the place where Haireena was sleeping. It seemed to me that she'd changed. She was still as beautiful as ever, but even more distant.

"It is good to have you back," I whispered. "Who'd have thought that my father would find Cleocatra's Kushion?"

"It is not Cleocatra's," hissed Haireena. "It is mine!"

And saying this she sprang up and grabbed an

arrow from her quiver.

My father has always made a point of telling me that we Kitons are good in a crisis. But he looked on in horror and cried out for Spitulus to help. Haireena leapt up onto the base of a statue.

"Cleocatra!" spat Haireena. "The enemy from Fleagypt. We will chase the invader from our lands."

Ever so slowly, Spitulus approached her.

"There are no invaders anymore," he said softly. "They left long ago."

"I will drive them out!" hissed Haireena and saying this she leapt down, unbarred the door and began to heave it open. There were cries from outside. It hadn't taken the Nomats long to find us.

Spitulus, my father and I sprang to the door to try to push it shut again.

Haireena picked up a spear and held it at my father's throat. "Obey me!" she cried. "I am your Queen."

"Wait!" said Spitulus.

"Why?" hissed Haireena.

"You cannot rule alone," said Spitulus. Look above you. And he pointed at two statues – a lion and a ram – they held up the world together.

I heaved my weight against the gate, but the many paws of the Nomats outside were stronger. It began to shift.

"You cannot rule alone. You must take a king," called Spitulus. "It is the law."

"One of you shall be my king," laughed Haireena. She swept her eyes around the room and I felt them settle on me. There was a time when I would have volunteered for a job like that, but not anymore.

"Not you!" she said catching my gaze. "You are far too young."

Spitulus had seen his chance and he padded slowly across to my side of the room. Then he leaned back against the door. I gasped as he took the weight.

"What is she doing?" I hissed.

"Choosing a king," he answered in a whisper.

"In the ancient times they would choose their kings from amongst the tribe. It might be the tallest, the strongest, the most handsome, the most war like..."

"You two!" cried Haireena. "You will fight for me." I gasped in horror. She was talking to Spitulus – and my father!

"You will not fight for her!" I hissed at father.

"Silence!" commanded Haireena.

"Obey me, or I'll have you thrown down the cliff as is the custom."

"That really was the custom," said Spitulus, his paws over his eyes.

"You should choose Spitulus," said a voice that had been unusually quiet. "Why don't you just take Spitulus here? He has youth on his side. He's bigger than me, stronger than me, the victor of one hundred battles in the arena. Isn't that right?" Spitulus nodded. "Why do we need to fight at all?"

"Because it pleases me," said Haireena, pushing the spear towards my father's throat.

"As you wish," said Spitulus. He picked up the sword and began to mark out a circle in the sand.

I felt sick. It is not every day that the female you love chooses your father above you to fight for her in a death match.

Spitulus passed the trident to my father and nodded. Father looked old and weak, as if he should be walking with a stick, not fighting with a spear.

"Begin!" said Haireena with a hiss. My father and Spitulus began to circle each other.

Haireena had picked up a bow and had a poison arrow already strung.

"Fight for me, I command it!" she cried.

Spitulus stepped in and aimed a blow at my fathers right side. Father stepped neatly away and blocked it with the trident.

"Fight properly!" hissed Haireena pointing the bow at me. "I do not want to watch a play fight."

The two gladiators circled each other.

"The gladus, verses the trident, always a most interesting challenge," said Spitulus. "One weapon has the superior reach," he said, aiming a couple of blows at my father to test the distance. "And yet, the other weapon has the advantage of speed!"

He let out a wild cry and charged at my father, his blade stabbing the air at eye level. It was a blow that could have split my father in two.

"Father!" I cried.

But my father was gone. It looked as if he was dancing on the sand, sweeping it with his tail. He gave a short leap forward and then shifted left. Then he stepped to the right and stumbled as if to fall. Spitulus' sword crashed to the stone floor.

I could not believe it. It must have been luck or something.

"Finish him!" commanded Haireena.

Father had Spitulus' sword pinned to the floor with his trident. Then the two exchanged a look.

He lunged forward and flipped the sword into the air. Spitulus caught it and the two turned upon Haireena as one. Spitulus snatched the bow from her paw and threw it to the ground.

All through the fight I had held the door back, but for a moment I must have forgotten to put my weight against it.

"Spitulus! The door!" I cried.

He leapt to my aid and threw his weight against it again but it was too late. The stone door lurched forward and many paws threw it open.

"Spartapuss!" cried a voice, "Thank Peus we're in time."

My father collects some strange friends and this one was no exception. He looked like some kind of Nomat himself as he was covered from nose to tail in sand.

"Eddipuss!" cried my father. "You're alive!" I

thought that the Nomats took you.

"We did," said a voice.

Five warriors sprang into the room. They were dressed in robes for desert travel and armed with knives and bows.

"We found this one wandering in the darkness, half-dead from thirst. It was hours before we could get any sense from him," said the first warrior.

"That does not surprise me," said my father. "I have exactly the same problem with him."

"I don't understand," I hissed. "What are you going to do to us?"

"We're not going to DO anything," laughed the warrior. "We've come with a message from Queen Kandmeet. She sends her greetings to the envoys of Nero."

We stood in silence. The warrior scratched his ear.

"You are the envoys of the Roman Emperor, are you not?"

SEPTEMBER X

September 10th

It falls to me to finish this tale. My son is not very good at finishing anything, apart from chicken suppers.

As we were soon to find out, there are 'Nomats' and 'Nomats'. That is to say, it seems that some of the desert tribes have rebelled against their Queen and seek to break the peace with Rome. They have been known to prey on travellers passing down the road.

So Kandmeet, which Spitulus say means 'Queen' in the Kushionite tongue, has her own band of warriors to protect the poor traveller. The last thing that the Queen wants is a war with Rome. She dare not give Nero any excuse to invade her land.

Within a week, we were safe in a village on route to the Queen's new capital at Merow. Ten days later we were relaxing in the palace. The royal doctors have taken poor Haireena off to treat her. Spitulus fears that it may be some time before she'll make a full recovery. Even the Queen's healers cannot say.

Although I can see why my son was interested in a female like Haireena, I am not sure that his mother would approve. Luckily he seems to be cured of love sickness. Perhaps it is because Haireena chose his aged father over him?

He was sad for a while. But now he is busy writing

songs on his new lyre to another female who he met on the journey. Her name is Misis – which is most unusual, as I believe that was also the name of the unfortunate camel that carried him on one part of his journey. I look forward to clearing this up with her when I meet her – the female that is, not the camel.

As for Spitulus and I, I'm delighted to record that we were granted an audience with the Queen of Kush. She is an imposing cat, no stranger to the cream bowl by the look of it. Her claws are filed into sharp points, and she had the luxurious fur of all of her nation.

As I approached her throne, she peered at me with amber eyes that were both playful and then serious.

"Welcome travellers," she purred. "My guards tell me your path in my kingdom has not been easy."

"That's right your majesty," said Spitulus. "But we are all the better for finding you at last."

"I hear that you are searching for treasure," purred the Queen. She hissed the word 'treasure' in a whisper that rose up to the carved ceiling of her hall.

"I have studied the lands of the Nile in books," said Spitulus. "I came to see them with my own eyes."

The Queen nodded, and turned her eyes on me.

"I am no scholar," I said. "I came looking for the thieves who stole my gold."

"Really?" she purred, lapping a little water from a silver bowl.

"I have no love of treasure Queen, but I had need of it, to buy the freedom of my son," I said.

"Our hospitality is famous. You shall have anything you need."

"My thanks Queen," I answered. "But I have no need of gold now. For I am reunited with my son."

"Good," said the Queen, smiling. "For you Spitulus, I have letters of introduction to give to my cousins beyond this land. If you seek the source of the Nile, that is where you will find it."

Spitulus bowed low. The Queen had sharp wits to match her filed claws. I remember thinking that she would have need of both to keep her kingdom free from the rule of Rome.

"Leave me now," she commanded. As we padded slowly down the steps, she called Spitulus back.

"When your Emperor asks about this land, what will you tell him?"

"I could tell him of its many great treasures..." began Spitulus.

The Queen let out a little hiss.

"Or, if your majesty wishes. I could tell him that it is a worthless dust-bowl, a blighted land containing nothing but sand."

The Queen's guards bristled and sprang forward. In an instant they'd unsheathed their curved blades. I feared that they'd cut him down where he stood.

"Well said Spitulus!" laughed the Queen. "If you are a true friend of the Kushionites, that is exactly what you will tell your Emperor. You are free to study our worthless land and wander anywhere you please.

As long as you promise to report back to me with your discoveries."

Spitulus bowed and padded off. I turned to follow.

"Stay a moment Spartapuss," said the Queen. "You don't need my gold but there is something that I must show you."

She led me through many doors and tunnels, down ladders and along narrow walkways that creaked and groaned as we passed. At last we came to a stone door, so large that it took ten guards to open it. When the door swung inwards, it revealed wonders worthy of the songs of my homeland – where the singers are not known for their understatement.

Great piles of gold, as high as Purramids dazzled my eyes. Precious stones were arranged in piles by order of size and by colour. There were a thousand treasures and yet I was drawn to the dark stone statues that stood in a ring around the outside of the hall.

"Why so many?" I asked.

"The ancients believed that the statues placed in this tomb could come to life and help the living," said the Queen.

"Why are you showing me?" I laughed.

"I didn't believe it either," said the Queen. "Until some years ago I found a statue of someone I once knew, standing here in this hall. Look carefully. Do you know anyone here?"

I padded around the room in a slow circle, looking at each statue in turn. There were kings and queens, warriors and slaves all standing in rows.

I stopped in the middle of a line, staring at a small statue. There was something familiar about her face.

"Tefnut!" I gasped.

There in stone, sat my old friend and teacher.

"Her name means 'water' in our tongue," said the Queen. "What do you know of her?"

I told the Queen the little that I knew of my old friend and mentor.

"I'm glad she helped you," said the Queen. "Good. The ancients will have ordered it. Now, perhaps you can help me? You possess something that was stolen from us long ago. Something that the ancients used in order to make these very statues. I must have it back and in exchange you may take any of these riches."

It was my turn to smile.

"Cleocatra's Kushion?" I asked. I pulled the old cushion from my bag. It was still caked in dust from the road and the stuffing had gone all hard.

"You can have it back my Queen," I said. "But may I beg a favour? Could I borrow it? I have a friend who can no longer use his eyes. I expect he could do with a sit down."

"That is not a good idea," said the Queen in horror.

"Why not?" I asked. "It made Jebel and Haireena well again."

"It only made them whole again. The Kushion heals them so they are ready to join the statues here in this hall. But it does not bring them back for long. Nothing in the world has the power to do that."

I nodded. Perhaps I'd need to find a different present for my wife.

"But I will send for your friend. There is a chance that my doctors can heal him," said the Queen.

I turned to leave, padding slowly back through the heaped treasures. Two flies buzzed around. One of them settled on a statue of a female warrior holding a golden bow. A lizard clung to the statue's beautiful face. With an echoing slap, it's long tongue darted out and caught the fly.

Startled at the noise, I span around and found myself face-to-face with the statue.

"Haireena!" I gasped.

Sitting by the statue's feet was a frog made of stone.

"I am so very sorry," said the Queen. "Perhaps you could tell your son that Haireena has decided to stay with me."

As I reached the entrance to the cave, the Queen called out to me.

"I hope your son will not be too upset."

"He'll understand," I answered. "He's done a lot of growing up recently."

As the guards met me at the foot of the steps, I heard the Queen's voice for the last time:

"Have you paid your driver yet? Send him to me."

The Spartapuss Series:

www.mogzilla.co.uk

I AM SPARTAPUSS

By Robin Price

In the first adventure in the Spartapuss series…
Rome AD 36. The mighty Feline Empire rules the world.
Spartapuss, a ginger cat is comfortable managing Rome's
finest Bath and Spa. But Fortune has other plans for him.
Spartapuss is arrested and imprisoned by Catligula, the
Emperor's heir. Sent to a school for gladiators, he must
fight and win his freedom in the Arena – before his oppo-
nents make dog food out of him.

'This witty Roman romp is history with cattitude.'
Junior Magazine (Scholastic)

ISBN 13: 978-0-9546576-0-4
UK £6.99
USA $14.95/ CAN $16.95

CATLIGULA

By Robin Price

'*Was this the most unkindest kit of all?*'

In the second adventure in the Spartapuss series...

Catligula becomes Emperor and his madness brings Rome
to within a whisker of disaster. When Spartapuss gets a job
at the Imperial Palace, Catligula wants him as his new best
friend. The Spraetorian Guard hatch a plot to destroy this
power-crazed puss in an Arena ambush. Will Spartapuss go
through with it, or will our six-clawed hero become history?

ISBN 978-0-9546576-1-1
UK £6.99
USA $10.95/ CAN $14.95

DIE CLAWDIUS

By Robin Price

'*You will die, Clawdius!*'

In third adventure in the Spartapuss series...

Clawdius, the least likely Emperor in Roman history, needs to show his enemies who's boss. So he decides to invade Spartapuss' home – The Land of the Kitons.
As battle lines are drawn, Spartapuss must take sides.
Can the magic of the Mewids help him to make the right choice?

'*Another fantastic story in this brilliantly inventive series. Any reader (young and old) will enjoy these books!*'
Teaching and Learning Magazine

ISBN 978-095-46576-8-0

UK £6.99   USA $10.95/ CAN $14.95

BOUDICAT

By Robin Price

'*This cat's not for turning, she's for burning!*"

In the fourth adventure in the Spartapuss series...

Queen Boudicat has declared war on Rome and she wants
Spartapuss to join her rebel army. Our ginger hero can't see
how a tiny tribe of Kitons can take on the mighty Feline
Empire. But warrior queens don't take 'No' for an answer.

*Action-packed and full of historical details, the Spartapuss
series follows the diary of a gladiator cat from Rome to the
Land of the Kitons (A.K.A. Britain). Boudicat, the fourth
book in the Spartapuss series, was awarded an 'Exclusively
Independent' pick of the month for July 2009.*

ISBN 978-190-61320-1-9
UK £6.99   USA $10.95/ CAN $14.95

LONDON DEEP

Story: Robin Price   *Artwork:* Paul McGrory

ISBN : 9781906132033   £7.99

London Deep is set in the future, in a flooded London - where
rival police forces for kids and adults compete to keep the peace.
Jemima Mallard is having a tough day. First two kids sank her
houseboat, and now the YPD (Youth Police) think she's mixed up
with a criminal called 'Father Thames'.

Mogzilla books are distributed in the UK by
Frances Lincoln Ltd.
Tel: +44 (0) 2072 844009
Fax: +44 (0) 2074 850490
Email: sales@frances-lincoln.com
Web: http://www.franceslincoln.com

For USA/ Canada orders contact:
Independent Publishers Group
Phone: 312.337.0747
http://www.ipgbook.com/